LAWLESS GUNS

Dudley Dean was the name Dudley Dean McGaughey used from the beginning for his series of exemplary Western novels written for Fawcett Gold Medal in the 1950s. McGaughey was born in Rialto, California, and began writing fiction for Street & Smith's *Wild West Weekly* in the early 1930s under the name Dean Owen. These early stories, and many more longer pulp novels written for Masked Rider Western and Texas Rangers after the Second World War, were aimed at a youthful readership. The 1950s marked McGaughey's Golden Age and virtually all that he wrote as Dudley Dean, Dean Owen, or Lincoln Drew during this decade repays a reader with rich dividends in tense storytelling and historical realism. This new direction can be seen in short novels he wrote early in the decade such as "Gun the Man Down" in *5 Western Novels* (August 1952) and "Hang the Man High!" in *Big-Book Western* (March 1954). They are notable for their maturity and presage the dramatic change in tone and characterization that occur in the first of the Dudley Dean novels, *Ambush At Rincon* (1953). *The Man From Riondo* (1954), if anything, was even better, with considerable scope in terms of locations, variety of characters, and unusual events. *Gun In The Valley* (1957) by Dudley Dean, *Chainlink* (1957) by Owen Evens, and *Rifle Ranch* (1958) by Lincoln Drew are quite probably his finest work among the fine novels from this decade. These stories are notable in particular for the complexity of their social themes and psychological relationships, but are narrated in a simple, straightforward style with such deftly orchestrated plots that their subtlety and depth may become apparent only upon reflection.

LAWLESS GUNS

Dudley Dean

GUNSMOKE

First published in the UK by Muller

This hardback edition 2009
by BBC Audiobooks Ltd
by arrangement with
Golden West Literary Agency

ISBN 978 1 405 68246 6

British Library Cataloguing in Publication Data available.

Printed and bound in Great Britain by
CPI Antony Rowe, Chippenham, Wiltshire

Chapter One

A MASS SQUAWKING of chickens could be heard this day by anyone passing Midway Store on the Paso Del Norte road. These sounds were followed by sudden quiet. Eight men, fired up by Texas whiskey, began to pluck the chickens they had killed. The birds belonged to Hugo Ortlander, and furnished eggs and stewing hens for the stage stop he owned. The extermination of his chickens brought no comment from Ortlander. He was a slightly built man who had survived in this tough country because of an unvarying neutrality in all things. However, he felt a strain on his principles because of what the men behind his store were planning for today.

The El Paso stage made its usual stop, but there was no hot meal for the passengers. Ortlander explained that his Mexican cook and her son, who odd-jobbed around the place, had run off when the bunch working over the chickens in the yard started to get liquored up. If the man this bunch were expecting didn't show up, they might take out their cruel humor on the two Mexicans. Such things were not uncommon.

The driver said through his beard, "If somebody killed all my chickens I'd bust their heads."

Ortlander spread his hands. "You run a place like this," he said in his small man's voice, "and you got to stay neutral. I can always buy more chickens."

The stage passengers grumbled about the lack of hot food. The stage pulled out.

5

The eight men sat on the ground behind the store, plucking the chickens. They put the feathers into two gunnysacks.

One of the men said, "Wish Ortlander had a feather mattress. Save us a lot of work."

"This ain't work, Dave," Ed Bates said. "This is pleasure when you think what we got planned for the turncoat." He sat on the ground, a bottle between his legs. He would drink and pull chicken feathers. He got some of the wet feathers stuck in his gray hair. He owned 66, a shirttail outfit over on Orion Creek. The gray in his mustache and beard was stained from tobacco juice. He wore the harassed look so common to Texas ranchers these days who had beef but no money. There was said to be a market opening in Kansas, but it took nerve to make the drive and a man could lose everything. Even the beef market in Chihuahua City was gone. A man didn't dare risk trailing a herd south because of the intense fighting between the forces of Juárez and Emperor Maximilian for control of the country. Poverty and indecision turned them sour and they struck out at those they could hate so easily.

Dave Franklin, owner of Spur, was Bates's nearest neighbor. He limped over to a washtub on a fire ring. He stuck a paddle in the black mass in the washtub.

"She's meltin', Ed," he called. He limped back and helped himself to a drink from his neighbor's bottle.

The other six men, who were so industriously drinking and plucking chickens, worked for the two ranchers. There was another man, Max Coleman, who did not drink nor did he bother with the chickens. He was foreman at 66, a dark, solidly built man. He kept watching the road that twisted up the lonely miles from the river.

"I recollect that those goose feathers is better for a job like this," one of the men said.

Ed Bates tilted back his head to take a drink. It threw his gaze on a level with the barn beside Midway Store. He frowned, made as if to cork the bottle, then reconsidered and had his drink.

"Dave, I was just rememberin' the time we helped Hugo raise that there barn," Bates said thickly.

"We drank a sight of beer," Dave Franklin said. "My kidneys ain't never been right since." Franklin laughed.

He wore his hat on the back of his head. He was forty-two, nearly twenty years younger than Ed Bates.

"I was rememberin' that Ralph Iverton loaned Hugo the money for this barn." Bates shifted on the ground and looked unhappy. "Ralph Iverton loaned us all a little here and there. It helped break him."

"I ain't forgot, Ed." Franklin stared down at his large hands, worn and hard from trying to keep together a two-bit spread in this first post-war year. "I also ain't forgot that Ralph heard Abe Lincoln's shoutin' way down here. And he walked off from his ranch and took his boy with him—"

"You reckon what we figure to do to the boy is right?" Bates said, wrinkling his weathered face.

"Well, if Ralph Iverton was still alive, I'd do it to him right along with his boy. I hate a turncoat worse'n I hate U.S. Grant."

"Ralph Iverton never fought against us."

"He didn't live long enough." Franklin's face darkened. "His boy fought against us. I got me a limp. Maybe Chase Iverton was the one pulled the trigger on me at Missionary Ridge."

The momentary reluctance Ed Bates had for the deed planned this day seemed to fade. The sacks were filled with feathers. They carried the dead chickens into the store. Hugo Ortlander put them in two huge pots which he placed on the stove.

"You'll eat chicken stew for a month," Bates said.

In the store with its shelves of tinned goods, counters with bolts of cloth, the deal tables, the short bar, they drank more whisky. From the beams hung saddles and ropes and about anything a man could need for ranching in this lonely end of God's world. Midway Store was the only place for supplies or recreation between San Carlos and Paso Del Norte. Here you could buy weapons, ammunition or a fast horse. Upstairs were rooms for overnight guests.

Ortlander's small face was worried. "I wish you boys'd pick somewheres else to do your devilment."

Nobody paid any attention to him. Ed Bates tried to adjust his gaze to the face of a battered bronze wall clock. It was four o'clock. It was nearly three hours since Chase Iverton had been seen heading toward Midway

Store for his monthly visit. The rider who had seen Iverton and his wife had spurred ahead. Bates and Franklin, who were already at Midway, grousing about the war and the poor cattle market, saw a chance to give vent to their frustrations.

One man said drunkenly, "We'll need brushes. You can't put him in the tub. You'll cook him."

"Cooked turncoat," Dave Franklin said. "Why not?"

"You got to brush the stuff on." Ed Bates turned to Ortlander. "You got some old brushes?"

"I'm neutral."

"That ain't what I asked you."

Franklin said, "Somebody go out back and look at that tar. We don't want it to boil over."

"We strip him nekkid in front of his wife," a man said. "Wonder how she'll like that."

"We'll have to hold her likely. She's got a she-cat temper."

"A good-looker. Damn, I get me an itch just thinkin' about her."

"I tell you what," Dave Franklin said, a strange hoarseness in his voice, "we oughta do the same to her."

"By God yes. Her the daughter of a Confederate hero and marryin' up with a turncoat."

"Strip her. Nekkid. Paint that purty skin with hot tar. Roll her in chicken feathers."

"I'd just like to roll her."

"She's the same as a back-room woman. She'd have to be to marry him."

"Boys, boys!" Hugo Ortlander tried to get their attention. "This thing is getting out of hand!"

"Shut up, Hugo. Or we won't even let you watch!" Franklin gave a drunken laugh.

Ed Bates turned to his foreman, Max Coleman. "You ain't drinkin', Max."

Coleman drew his gun and checked the loads. Somehow the professional ease with which this man had performed the act sobered the onlookers somewhat.

Ed Bates squinted at his foreman's dark face. "You got somethin' planned on your own, Max?"

Coleman gave him a hard smile. He went to the porch and stood looking south along the road that Chase Iverton would take from his Flatiron ranch.

Le320

Somebody said, "I hear Coleman lost two brothers."

"I heard it was three," Franklin said. "They was with Pickett."

Ed Bates stood in deep thought for a moment, then made his decision. "The woman ain't to be touched."

"Aw, Ed. I ain't had me a look at a woman for six months."

"Go to Ruby's Place in San Carlos an' do your lookin'. Boys, I mean it." Bates looked around at the men. Nobody said anything for a moment.

"Her pa the colonel dead in a stinkin' Yank prison," Franklin said heavily. "She's no good or she'd have more feelin' for his memory than to marry a traitor."

"You got to say this for Iverton," Hugo Ortlander put in. "It took guts for him to come back to ranchin' here. Seein' as how much he's hated."

"Hugo, we'll get your place here talked about from Kansas to Chihuahua City," Franklin said. "Folks'll spread the word that Midway Store is where they seen a man and a woman wearin' nothin' but tar and chicken feathers. We'll keep 'em here till the eastbound comes through tomorrow."

Hugo Ortlander's small face tightened. "You're crazy drunk. The lot of you!"

"Drunk on your whisky that we paid for, Hugo!"

"Bad enough to plan this for a man. But a woman— You're not goin' to do this foul thing!"

Ortlander tried to reach a revolver he kept on the backbar. One of the men got him from behind with a thick forearm around the neck.

"Just stand hitched, Hugo," the man warned, "or we'll let daylight into your head."

Max Coleman's voice came sharply from the veranda. "Here they come!"

"Hugo, where's them goddam brushes?" Franklin demanded.

Ortlander, his face purple from the forearm squeezing his throat, said nothing.

One of the men had been rummaging in the back room. "I got 'em!" he cried triumphantly.

"I bet when we peel down them Ivertons," Franklin said, "that she's as yellow underneath as her turncoat husband!"

Chapter Two

ALL THE WAY from his Flatiron ranch the spring wind bit coldly at Chase Iverton's wide shoulders as it swept up from Mexico, through the passes of the Chisos and at last into these hills of the Bend. He licked grit from the corners of his long mouth. A sigh built up in the tough body, for ahead he could see the roof of Midway Store. The journey was nearly over. And it had been safely made.

His fingers were stiff from the cold and from holding the reins of the team. "We didn't even catch sight of a Comanche," he said to his wife.

"Or catch sight of a neighbor." Her blue eyes were bitter.

"A neighbor's more to be feared than a redman." He gave a slow shake of his head. He tipped back his hat. His brown hair was a rust color when seen in certain lights. He was twenty-six years old and sometimes he thought that the heaviest burden in all of Texas rested on his shoulders.

"What can you expect but hate from your neighbors?" Marie demanded crossly. "You didn't choose sides wisely in the war."

He slanted his gray eyes at her. They were bloodshot from the strain of watching both sides of the wagon road that curved from his ranch near the river all the way to Midway Store. "The fact that I was Union," he reminded, "didn't keep you from marrying me."

She said nothing to this, but snuggled deeper into an old gray cloak. The collar was turned up around her pretty face to shield it from the wind. She had clumsily patched a rip in the garment with green cloth. "I wish this damn wind would stop."

The oath annoyed him. It was a symbol of her discontent. "I thought that fancy school in St. Louis was supposed to make a lady out of you."

"What I learned at Miss Larrabee's is of no value now.

10

There are no ladies. No gentlemen. The war changed all that."

His back stiffened in the brush jacket he wore, straining the fabric. For most of the twenty miles from Flatiron they had argued. And the argument was not dead.

"If you thought anything of me at all," Marie snapped, "you'd move us to Cross Hammer where we'd have a decent roof over our heads."

"I'll manage Cross Hammer for you," he said, weary of advancing the same old arguments. "But I won't live there. We'll continue to live at Flatiron."

"With Poppa dead it's my ranch. We could be happy there—"

"Sometimes I wonder if you even have the capacity for happiness."

She settled deeper into the old gray cloak. Ahead they could see the store buildings plainly now. Chase drove onto the Paso road. Beyond the two-story frame store building were two other structures, a barn and a blacksmith shop.

As they made the turn a blast of wind struck them in the face.

"The wind never seemed to blow nearly as hard at Cross Hammer." There was an edge to her voice.

"You keep at a man, don't you?"

"I just want a few comforts." The tip of her nose was sunburned. She was not a tall girl, but well-formed. At first glance she seemed fragile. Possibly because of her finely molded features. Her light blue eyes, however, mirrored an inner strength, and also the discontent that Chase had noticed growing since their marriage six months ago.

As they approached the store he saw Max Coleman on the veranda. A rising tension claimed Chase. He had come all this way without incident. Two months ago he had whipped Coleman. There had been other fights. He'd come home one day and found "Turncoat" painted in red letters on his barn wall. His nerves were getting short. He'd known it wouldn't be easy coming back here. But so far they hadn't let up on him at all.

"I hope you don't have to whip *him* again," Marie said, nodding at Coleman. She was untying a faded green scarf knotted under her chin.

"I'm getting tired of having to prove myself around here," Chase said. Shifting the reins to his left hand he removed the canvas covering from the cedar-butted .44 at his belt. He hoped the covering had been sufficient to keep out dust and sand during the drive from Flatiron. From the way Coleman stood, his heavy body rigid, Chase sensed trouble. He might need that gun.

Chase tied the team to a stump. On the ground he seemed even taller. He was an inch over six feet. On his face, brown as the wide leather belt around his waist, were lines of pressure at eyes and mouth. His nose was slightly off center, the result of a glancing blow from a Rebel rifle butt in hand-to-hand combat.

Chase looked up at Coleman on the porch. "Don't try and climb my back today," he warned the 66 foreman. "I'm through with fist fighting." He put a hand significantly on the butt of his gun.

Marie was sniffing the air. "What smells?"

"Chicken," Chase said, and lifted his voice. "Hey, Hugo! Chicken for supper tonight?" Then Chase broke off, scowling. Mingled with the aroma of stewing chickens was a pungent odor he couldn't place at the moment. "Hugo!" he called again.

There was no answer.

A warning bell clanged in his mind. He looked around. An unnatural quiet hung over Midway Store. Evelina should be rushing out to kiss him on both cheeks. And her son, Pablo, ought to be taking the horses to the barn—

Then the odor registered. Hot tar.

He shot Coleman a glance, saw the faint smile on the foreman's lips. Chase stepped back. "Marie, get inside!"

Four men came at a dead run from the west side of the store. And as Chase whirled to meet them, somebody hurled a rock that caught him between the shoulder-blades. With the breath driven out of him, he fell. The gun he had half-drawn, slipped from his fingers. Then they were on him, pinning arms and legs. Three of them wrenched him to his feet. A noose dropped over his head, pinning his arms to his sides.

His hat was gone, his rust-colored hair powdered with dust. They took several turns with the rope about his arms. There was a strange quiet now and the men were looking at Marie. As men will look who drunkenly anticipate some forbidden pleasure.

Coleman touched Marie on the arm. "This way, ma'am." He nodded toward the rear yard.

"What does this mean!" Marie looked frightened.

"It means we're goin' to peel you down, ma'am," Coleman said. "We're goin' to run you an' that turncoat husband of yours outa Texas."

There was shock in Marie's blue eyes. She looked across the yard where her husband stood with his arms roped to his sides. His mouth was a white line across his dark face. He looked around. They were all drunk—you could tell that at one glance. They reeked of Ortlander's hill-distilled whisky. Only one man appeared sober. Max Coleman.

"You and me alone, Coleman," Chase said through his white teeth. "With a gun. Or are you gutless enough to fight me through my wife!"

"The gun can come later." Coleman caught Marie by the wrists, pulled her arms behind her.

Chase let his gaze slide to Ed Bates. The old rancher stood with gray head bowed, looking at the ground. He staggered, shifted his weight. It was hard for Chase to remember that his father and this man had been fast friends.

"You've got a wife, Ed," Chase said. "Your married daughter lives in Austin. You'd like this to happen to your women folks?"

Ed Bates licked at his dirty uncut beard, and looked at the men. "Boys, I got no use for a man fights against his own people. But the woman didn't fight."

Dave Franklin limped over to where Chase stood, surrounded. "You an' Marie Herrick was cozy before the war. I remember. Her pa must've had second sight about how you'd turn out. He hated your bleedin' guts even then."

"Get the brushes ready, boys," Coleman said. He pushed Marie around the side of the building. Some of them trailed along. A few of the men stood around Ed Bates.

Bates said, "We leave the woman alone."

Dave Franklin looked back. "Ed, you're out-voted."

They shoved Chase to the rear yard. Coleman had turned Marie loose. She stood near the tub of hot tar that smoked on the fire ring. Three old brushes lay on the ground near the sacks of chicken feathers.

Chase let his gaze swing around the group of men who seemed strangely silent now. As if waiting for one of their number to dip the first brush in the tub, to pick up the first handful of chicken feathers.

"Remember this." Chase Iverton's voice shook slightly. "I'm going to kill any man who puts a hand on my wife." He looked at each flushed face in turn. "If I've got to kill the lot of you I will."

"She's as guilty as you are," Franklin said.

"Guilty because she loves a man and marries him?" His eyes were cold as winter ice in the Chisos. "The war's over, haven't you heard? That the hate and bitterness can be eliminated by a little common sense—"

"All this bitterness wiped out when Lee polished up his sword for Grant's scabbard," Franklin said, his lips twisting. "We forget about it easy as that."

"None of it was easy. The decision I made to fight to preserve the Union wasn't easy."

"If her pa the colonel could come back from the dead," Franklin said, "he'd hang you higher'n a summer moon."

"I expect he'd try." Chase gave him a long look. "If you've got to do this thing, do it to me. Alone. Don't degrade yourselves by touching her."

The men shifted uncomfortably.

Marie's blue eyes were bright with anger. "If you don't respect me, at least respect the memory of my father. They say he died a hero. I hear there's talk of erecting a statue to him in San Carlos. You'll blacken his memory with this sort of act you plan."

"You beggin' for yourself, ma'am?" Coleman's voice came thinly across her shoulder. "Or for your husband."

Marie said, "I can tell you this. If my father was alive he'd hang every man here."

"But your pa ain't alive, ma'am. If he was you sure as hell wouldn't be married to Chase Iverton."

"Amen to that," Franklin said.

Chase cast a sidelong glance to the man on his left. The man held a coil of rope. The other end of the rope

had been wrapped around Chase's arms. It was not tied.
Just the wrapping of the rope.

Suddenly he spun away from the man holding the
rope. Whirling his body in such a way that the lashings
came free of his arms. And at the same moment Marie
pivoted and twisted free of Coleman's grasp. Her finger-
nails tore at Coleman's eyes. With a hoarse cry of alarm
he fell back, desperately trying to defend himself.

Before any of the drunken men nearest Chase could
react, he flexed his arms and loosened the noose holding
his arms. But he could not get it over his head before a
man slammed into him. Chase fell, skinned his knees. He
dodged a kick aimed at his head. He lunged upward,
smashing a man in the face with one hand, tearing free
the man's belt gun with the other.

Wheeling, he saw that Coleman had thrown Marie to
one side. Coleman's gun came out. Through the dust
kicked up·by the skirmish there appeared a finger of
orange-colored flame. The harsh sound of exploding pow-
der. Another shot, whistling after the first, but from
Chase Iverton's gun. Coleman's weapon skated across
the yard. Coleman stood as if drunk for a moment, sway-
ing he was staring stupidly down at his right wrist that
was pumping blood all over the front of his trousers.

Chase backed up a step, his revolver cocked. The men
turned woodenly from watching the suffering Coleman.

"I didn't aim for the wrist," Chase said. "I intended to
kill him. Next time I'll make sure of my aim. Get your
horses. Get out of here. I mean it!"

The men looked at the gun. Marie had picked herself
up. Angrily she brushed dust from her clothing. "You're
a pack of wild animals!" she cried.

A shaft of white bone was jutting from Coleman's
wrist. He made low sounds of pain. Ed Bates bandaged
the wrist with a bandanna. They managed to get the
foreman into the saddle. The group that had been so
hilarious but a few minutes before now seemed strangely
subdued.

Ed Bates halted his horse at the edge of the yard. "It
was wrong to get your wife roped in on this, Chase. But
reckon you know we don't feel kindly toward you."

"Clear out, Ed. Take your dogs with you!"

"If you got the brains of a loco gnat you'll get out of Texas!"

"I came back to raise Texas beef. To sell Texas beef. I intend raising my family here. Don't anybody try and pull a stunt like this again!"

Chase recovered his own revolver. He threw the gun he had lifted from a holster across the yard to the man who owned it. They rode out, a hangdog look about them. They did not look back.

Chapter Three

CHASE FOUND Hugo Ortlander locked up in a storeroom. The little man soundly cursed Bates and Franklin and their men. "They were drunk, Chase. Or they'd have never tried a thing like that."

"Sometimes I wonder what I used for brains," Chase said wearily. "In thinking I could come back here and make a life for myself."

"If you hadn't come back, you and Marie wouldn't be married."

"No." Chase took a moment to add, "Life wouldn't mean very much without her. I'm a lucky man."

He looked across the room where Marie sat at a deal table, fussing with her pale hair. Ortlander had given her some hot coffee. Now he went to fill the list of supplies Chase gave him.

Chase poured himself a drink from the bottle Ortlander set out. He was thankful there were no other customers in the big barn-like building. He would be spared further baiting. For the time being at least. The business today had shaken him. He wondered if Coleman would ever again have the full use of his right arm. At the moment he didn't care very much. A split second of timing, off either way and Coleman would be dead. Or he, Chase Iverton, would be dead and leave a weeping widow.

He looked at Marie's yellow head, wondering how

much weeping she would do at his grave. He had known her since she was eight or nine. Sometimes he felt as if he didn't know her at all.

He remembered the first week he was home from the war and how quickly the news spread. Marie was the only one who hadn't called him "turncoat." She drove down that first week to Flatiron in a buckboard, escorted by four cowhands from her late father's vast Cross Hammer ranch. The riders were the only ones left out of a crew of twenty.

"Welcome home, Chase," she had said that day. Then, weeping, she came into his arms. "Poppa's dead. In a Yankee prison. Chase, I'm so alone. You're all I've got."

And that day Chase said, "What about Paul?"

"He's just like a brother. Besides, he didn't come back from the war."

Chase felt a sadness that his old rival for Marie's hand was gone. He and Paul Dublin had been boys together here in this rough country of the Bend.

Chase said, "All through the war I never stopped thinking of you, Marie."

"Come to visit me at Cross Hammer. There's nothing there but cattle you can't sell and old men and—" She wept again.

The following month they drove all the way to San Carlos to be married. There they had their first quarrel because he wouldn't go to live at Cross Hammer. But how could he explain that he would never live in a house where the name Iverton had been so hated? Where her father would rather have cupped his hand around the head of a rattlesnake than shake the hand of an Iverton. Her father, Josh Herrick, had so stated many times.

Chase ran Cross Hammer only for Marie. When Texas beef became valuable—which he hoped it would—the ranch could be sold. Every dollar would be banked in Marie's name.

During their stay in San Carlos Chase had been forced to defend himself on three occasions. One of his assailants suffered a broken arm, another remained unconscious for two days. The third screamed when Chase's bullet was dug out of his leg. And this was supposed to be a honeymoon.

Chase walked over and sat down at the deal table. Marie had finished pinning up her hair. "It was a long hard trip," he said. "I imagine you're tired."

"If we lived at Cross Hammer we'd be much closer to everything."

He clenched his teeth. It had been said so many times before, why say it again? How his father and Colonel Josh Herrick had been such bitter enemies. How could he make her understand that he wanted to be his own man, build his own life. That was why he had returned to Texas. It was a challenge. Flatiron ranch was his and the cattle that ran on it. If he refused to claim his birthright he was a coward and he would be forever running from himself.

Her composure after the harrowing experience of the day nettled him. "Those boys intended getting pretty rough with you. Don't you feel a little shaky?"

"There are worse things than being tarred and feathered." She shrugged. "They didn't intend killing me. That's about all that would frighten me."

"You're a strange woman. You baffle me."

Because he wanted to get away from her he took the team to the barn and grained them. It seemed a lifetime ago that he and his father had spent a week here at Midway and helped Hugo Ortlander raise this structure. A warmth came over him for this reminded him of his boyhood, so distant now it seemed as if it had been lived by someone else.

Ortlander came to the barn. He said again he was sorry about what had happened today. Chase said nothing.

"You and Paul Dublin were friends before the war," Ortlander said.

"Friends except where it came to Marie," Chase said with a sad smile. "Even then I suppose our rivalry was friendly enough. I guess Paul didn't make it back from the war."

"He's hangin' around Mesilla," Ortlander said.

"Thank God he's alive."

"Lettin' him live through the war," Ortlander said in his small voice, "is one place God used poor judgment."

Chase turned from the feed bin. "Paul was always a little wild, but you can't condemn a man—"

"He's gone bronc. Runnin' with some of the old Cross Hammer crew that went to war with the colonel. They're killers."

Chase felt his mouth tighten. "Thanks for not saying anything in front of Marie. She thought a lot of him. The colonel took him in years back, remember, and raised him."

Ortlander looked toward the door as if to see if anyone was within earshot. The big barn was empty, save for the two men and the horses. "Chase, I get some tough boys through here. Boys that have their ear to the ground."

"So?"

"One of 'em come through here last week." Ortlander looked grim. "He claimed he heard the colonel ain't dead."

Chase watched a spider scurry up the barn wall. For a moment he was shocked, then he relaxed. This was one rumor that was false. Marie had received a letter from the commandant of Lake Prison near Chicago that her father had succumbed to battle wounds while a prisoner of war. "I've faced everything else, Hugo. I can face the colonel coming home. Provided it's true. Which I doubt."

"I ain't told anybody else about this, Chase."

"You take my part as much as you can. I appreciate it."

"Your pa was my best friend. I didn't always agree with him, but—"

"He was a dreamer," Chase said. "He believed in mankind. The war broke his heart."

"One thing he did I always agreed with." Ortlander gave Chase a grim smile. "The time he beat the livin' hell out of Marie's pa right here at Midway."

An old bitterness touched Chase's eyes. "He never forgave my father for that humiliation. He never forgave me for being son to my father."

"The worst thing you can do to a thief like Colonel Herrick," Ortlander said gravely, "is to call him one to his face like your pa done. Some folks hereabouts think it's a joke that Marie's pa stole every section of Cross Hammer from the Arguellos."

"Stealing from Mexicans seems to be a prime sport," Chase said bitterly.

"I hear you've got one of the Arguello boys workin' for you."

"The last Arguello on this side of the line." Chase sighed. "In fact, he's the only hand I could hire."

"They'll forget this turncoat business around here one of these days."

Chase took a long moment in answering. "It does something to a man to see people he's raised with go crazy like that bunch did today. Bad enough they'd want to pour their hot tar and chicken feathers on me. But my wife—"

Ortlander stared at the hard and bitter face of the younger man. "I got a feelin' the war has changed us all. That nothin' will ever be the same again."

"Marie shares that feeling."

"What you reckon she will say if her pa really does come home?"

Chase stared out the wide doorway of the barn where fading sunlight touched tall cottonwoods across the road. This possibility that the colonel might be alive was one thing he had not considered. That was impossible, he told himself. The colonel was in his grave. But still the nagging doubt was there in the back of his mind.

"There wasn't much love between Marie and her father," Chase said. "It's hard to say just how she would feel if he came home."

They returned to the store. Marie had removed her patched gray cloak and put it over the back of her chair. Her faded blue dress fit snugly under the arms.

"Got some new dress goods in last week," Ortlander told her and waved a hand at a table where bolts of cloth were piled.

"I might be interested," Marie said. "If I could sew." She gave Chase a petulant sidelong glance. "Or if I could afford a seamstress."

Chase felt his ears redden. Despite her apparent lack of interest Marie went over to examine the cloth.

Chase and Marie ate stewed chicken for supper. They sat at a table, their backs to the wall. A few men drifted in, had drinks and left. They were strangers, for which Chase was thankful. He'd had about enough baiting for one day. It was prudent, he knew, to sleep away from Midway tonight. But Marie was tired from the long trip.

And he decided to risk a return of Bates and Franklin and their men. One thing for sure, Max Coleman wouldn't be interested in further action tonight. Not with that wrist.

Chase paid Ortlander for the meal, the room they would occupy tonight and also for the breakfast they would eat before starting the long trip home with their supplies.

Upstairs Chase locked their door on the inside and undressed down to his underwear. Marie was already in bed. He lay in the darkness a moment, listening to the night sounds, the hoot of an owl, the stomp of horses in the barn next door. "What if your father should prove to be alive and not dead?" he said suddenly.

He felt her stir beside him. "Poppa's dead. The Union Army wrote me— What made you say a thing like that?"

"He wouldn't be happy to find us married."

She sat up in bed. Moonlight filtering through the window touched her long pale hair. "How he feels about my marriage wouldn't interest me at all. I hated him."

"That's no way to talk," he said sharply.

"And you also hated him. And so did your father. Those scars on Poppa's face. Your father put them there. Poppa carried those scars to his grave."

"There was so much hate between our families. Why did you marry me?"

She was silent a moment. Then she said, "That's a fool question. I love you."

"Maybe I was first home from the war. Maybe that's why you married me."

She lay down on his arm. "I'd be real wifely if you'd promise to move us to Cross Hammer."

He felt the old wound reopen. "I came home to make my life at Flatiron. You agreed to share that life."

"If we lived at Cross Hammer we'd be much nearer town. And if I needed a doctor—for having a baby—"

"If that happens I'll move you to San Carlos. That I promise.

With a sigh of exasperation she turned her back on him. This angered him. Pressures had been building. This taking of a young and pretty wife had complicated his life. He caught her roughly by the shoulders and kissed her. "Don't ever turn from me again. You hear?"

She drew back and looked at him. "Why don't you be rough with me more often?"

He tried to gauge the strange, breathless sound of her voice. "I don't live that way, Marie. I'm not breaking a horse. I want to treat a woman gentle. I want her to love me and respect me for myself. I don't like this constant game we have to play."

"This coming to Midway is a sort of holiday for us," she whispered. "I guess we should make the most of it."

Tired as he was sleep did not come easily. He wondered how it had been between his father and mother. Was there this constant warfare? He had never known a woman around the house. His mother had died at his birth. And his father was buried in Illinois, so there was no asking him.

Chase lay in the quiet darkness, wondering what their lives would mean in the years to come. His victory tonight—if it could be called that—seemed empty and without meaning.

Chapter Four

EARLIER THAT DAY, at twilight, two horsemen had pushed east along the Paso road. The older of the pair looked upon Texas for the first time in more than four years. The other one was seeing Texas for the first time.

This man rode with bandanna across the lower part of his long face. "The wind always blow like this in Texas, Colonel?"

"Sometimes it's worse," Colonel Josh Herrick grunted through his own bandanna. His narrow-brimmed, fawn-colored hat was anchored under his chin by a lanyard. There was about his black suit a look of newness despite the faint shine on back of coat and trousers from rubbing against stage coach seats during the long trip south from Chicago. His shirt had originally been white. Now it was a shade of gray from dust and perspiration. At his belt he carried a .38 caliber officer's gun.

"These horses are about done," his companion said.

"Horses are the cheapest damn thing in Texas, Luke. That's something you'll learn."

Luke Benreed turned his tall, solid frame slightly in the saddle to peer at the older man. "I heard Texas beef was the cheapest thing," he said with a laugh.

"Not now." The colonel slapped at a money belt. "Not since I got my Yankee beef contract." The colonel's black eyes were hard. "This contract will change a lot of things, Luke. For one thing it'll bring my daughter home."

"What if she won't come?"

"She'll come. One way or another."

Even thinking of his daughter put a white fire through him. He thought of the months in the prison hospital, not knowing whether he would live or die. Or caring very much. When he was finally recovering, the war was over and he learned that through some mixup in records, his daughter had been notified that he was dead. Just as he was about to rectify this error, the letter had come from Paul Dublin: Marie had gotten married to Chase Iverton.

It was a worse blow than the Yankee bullet that had nearly claimed his life. Let her think me dead, he decided. It will be small payment for this treachery.

The weeks of convalescence brought him luck, for he became the friend of a Union captain who owned an interest in a packinghouse. When this friend learned the colonel had beef but no market, they became partners.

Now at last Colonel Josh Herrick was on his way home. He would get his old Cross Hammer crew, made up of the tough young men who had ridden off with him to war. The crew had been hanging around Mesilla with Paul Dublin. Upon his release from the hospital the colonel had written Paul at the Mesilla address, ordering him to bring the crew to Cross Hammer on the fifteenth of the month. The fifteenth was two days away.

Luke Benreed's yellow eyes slanted a look at the colonel. "Hope we don't have to sleep out again tonight."

"We won't. We'll stop at Midway Store. Five miles or so ahead."

"Good. I can do with a hot meal." Benreed rode tall in the saddle. He had been in the colonel's outfit during the war and had been captured with him. He had come immediately when the colonel wrote and offered him a job. The colonel needed tough men. Benreed considered himself capable of filling that requirement.

At last the yellow glow of lamplighted windows appeared ahead. The colonel and Benreed left their horses at the rail. One of Ortlander's Mexicans could take care of them.

When the colonel saw the familiar room in all its familiar disorder he felt for the first time that he was home.

Hugo Ortlander was behind his bar. There was no one else in the place. The colonel and Benreed walked the length of the room. Ortlander seemed to have shrunk in stature since they entered. His face lost color and his gaze shot toward the ceiling.

"I'm not a ghost, if that's what's worrying you," the colonel said. He did not offer his hand. "This here's Luke Benreed. He'll be segundo at Cross Hammer."

"Howdy," Ortlander said in a small voice, and set out bottles and glasses.

"Paul Dublin will be my foreman," the colonel said. He sniffed the air. "We'll have some of that chicken you've got cooking."

Ortlander lost even more color, for Luke Benreed had walked over to a chair and picked up a gray cloak. His yellow eyes were shining. "I need whisky, food and what goes with this coat."

"Hugo's usually got a woman hanging around," the colonel said. "Go get her, Hugo."

Ortlander's eyes were very large. "Yeah—yeah I'll go upstairs and see what I can do."

The colonel looked casually at the cloak Benreed had slung over his arm. He looked again.

"Hold it, Hugo," he said crisply.

The little man had been about to scamper up the stairway behind the bar. Now he turned.

The colonel's black eyes were hard. "I gave my daughter a cloak like this. Before the war."

Ortlander lifted both small hands in protest. "Don't do nothin', Colonel. Kee-ryst, I've had enough trouble here for one day!"

The colonel stood as if transfixed. "By God," he breathed. "They're here! Under this roof!"

Chase heard quiet steps in the hallway. The footsteps paused before his door. Alerted, he slipped out of bed. In this post-war Texas a man lived constantly with danger.

Quickly he drew his revolver from the belt looped over a chairback. A tall figure in long woolen underwear, he moved behind the door just as it crashed inward. The glow of a lantern filled the room. Two men surged in.

The shorter of the pair held the lantern. His companion, thick through neck and shoulder, held a revolver pointed at the terrified girl on the bed.

The short one with the lantern stormed up to the bed where Marie was sitting up, her face seemingly as colorless as the whitewashed walls.

Chase stepped behind the big man. "Gents, you're in the wrong room!"

And at that moment he recognized the man with the lantern as Marie screamed, "Poppa!"

At the sound of Chase's voice Luke Benreed started to pivot. Before he could cover the man behind him, he was hit a solid smash on the head by a downswinging gunbarrel. Benreed fell heavily and did not move.

Chase leveled the gun at the colonel. "So you really did make it back from the dead."

"You fiend!" the colonel cried. "You dirty fiend! You and her. In this room together!"

"She's my wife!" Chase lowered the revolver.

The lantern in the colonel's hand trembled. He set down the lantern on the floor and tried to grab the .38 caliber officer's revolver at his belt. But Chase slammed into him, wrested the weapon from his fingers and threw it on the bed.

"Poppa, why didn't you write?"

"I heard you and this—this Iverton were married. I decided to surprise you."

"That you've done," Chase admitted.

The man on the floor stirred. There was blood at the roots of his dark hair.

The colonel said, "That's my new foreman. Benreed. You've made a bad enemy, Iverton."

Marie said, "Get out, Poppa, and leave us alone."

"I've got a beef contract, Marie." The colonel held out a hand to his daughter. "I'll be the biggest man in this corner of Texas. You can go back to Miss Larrabee's and finish your schooling—"

"I've had quite enough of Miss Larrabee's."

"Then we'll make other plans. Marie, get your clothes on. We'll turn our backs."

Chase Iverton's mouth hardened. "I'm afraid you're getting things twisted. Marie is your daughter, and I'll respect that. But she's also my wife."

"Not for long!" Saliva burst from the colonel's bearded lips. "Marie, I'll give you all the money you want—"

"You never spent any money on me in your life, Poppa."

"I sent you to a good school in St. Louis—"

"Only to get me out of the way so you could go fight your war and not have to worry about me."

Luke Benreed got shakily to his feet. He started for the gun he had dropped. Chase kicked it under the bed.

"Get out of here!" Chase ordered. "Both of you!"

The colonel's tongue licked at the beard around his lips. "Marie, I'm your father. You come home."

"I'm glad you're alive and not dead," Marie told him. "But you're not ordering me. Not now. I have a husband."

The colonel fumed and cursed, but in the end Chase herded them both downstairs. He saw that Hugo Ortlander lay behind his bar, gagged, wrists and ankles roped. The little man's angry gaze stabbed the colonel and Benreed.

Holding the pair covered Chase got a knife from behind the bar and freed Ortlander. The little man got up, pulling at his gag.

"They got the drop on me, Chase," he said, feeling the raw corners of his mouth where the gag had cut. "It was my fault. I opened my mouth at the wrong time."

Chase forced the colonel and Benreed into the saddles of the spent horses tied in front of the store. He pulled free their booted rifles and threw them into the brush beside the store.

"These horses are about done," Benreed said, fingering the cut on his head. "Let us switch saddles—"

"The hell with you," Chase said through his teeth.

"Your pa tried to fight me!" the colonel cried. "He went broke. You'll do worse than that. I'll bury you here!" Chase gestured with the revolver and they headed east at a lope. The wind cut through his underwear. His teeth were chattering.

Despite the lateness of the hour Chase loaded his wagon with the supplies he had come for. He and Marie drove south in the Flatiron wagon. Twice this day their luck had held at Midway Store. There was no use in stretching it too thin.

"This sort of complicates our lives," Chase soberly told his wife as they drove through the darkness. The wind had died down. A new moon was bright over the Chisos. "But thanks for taking my part against your father."

"Did you doubt that I'd stay with you?"

"Your father claims he'll be a rich man."

The team slowed, settled into their collars as the road climbed steeply through the dark and lonely hills."

"*We'll* be rich, Chase," Marie said. "There'll be some way for us to get rich. You wait and see."

"Getting rich isn't all there is to life."

"It's most of life." She gave a toss of her head. "Poppa deserted me once too often. I think he knows it now."

"You should visit him. After all, he is your father."

"Honey, how soon can we add on rooms to the house? And get a woman to do the house chores?"

"Soon, I hope." He patted her knee. "We're going to have a tough fight but we'll make it." He wished he really felt as confident as he tried to sound. The odds against his success here—his even staying alive, for that matter—had increased perceptibly with the return of Colonel Josh Herrick from the dead.

Five miles south of Midway Store they pulled off the road and into a thicket. Marie slept on the ground until dawn. Chase sat beside her, a rifle across his knees. He had the feeling that from now on many nights would be spent with a loaded gun at hand.

For the next several days Chase and his hired hand, Miguel Arguello, split up the night on guard duty. But the colonel made no move against Flatiron. Arguello, slender, dark, mustached, had taken the news that the colonel was alive and not dead with less display of emotion than Chase felt he was entitled to show. After all, the colonel had stolen Cross Hammer from some of Arguello's relatives.

They spent the days breaking horses in the circular stone corral. They worked the roughness out of the twenty-five head of horses Chase had purchased cheap along the river. He intended trailing them to Fort Ellenden in New Mexico for sale as cavalry remounts. His contact there was a Major Jackson he had met in the war.

Arguello was a fine horseman and Chase told him so after the second week passed with no trouble. Arguello came up from the breaking corral one day, after a hard session with a fractious dun. He picked up his sawed-off shotgun—his favorite weapon—which he carried in a special saddle scabbard when riding. This weapon, Arguello claimed, was equal to a small army if it was used up close.

"Thanks for sticking with me through this, Miguel," Chase said. "I wouldn't blame you much if you went to Mexico with the rest of your family."

"You think I am afraid because this colonel is back from the dead?" He patted the sawed-off shotgun under his arm. "I would like very much to use this on him."

Chase soberly regarded the dark face. "I don't have much use for him either, Miguel. But after all, he is my wife's father."

Chase did the cooking. Marie had made several attempts but they turned out tragically. She seemed to resent the fact that Arguello took his meals with them. Chase supposed she couldn't be blamed for sharing her father's hatred of Mexicans. After all, she had been brought up in such an atmosphere. But his patience in trying to get her to change her viewpoint gradually wore thin. One night she said she'd be glad when they could get a regular crew and let Arguello go. She didn't like having a Mexican in the house.

"Can't you understand your father's hatred?" he demanded. "You steal from a man and you learn to hate him. I suppose you'd think it was all right if somebody stole this ranch from us."

"Honey, you'd fight them." She smiled. "You're strong. People are a little afraid of you."

"Nobody's afraid of me."

"You think not? That man Coleman you shot. He's supposed to be pretty fast with a gun. Yet you beat him. Don't worry. I hear the talk, even if you don't."

"What talk?"

"Paul said—"

He felt a stiffness in his shoulders. "Paul Dublin?" And when she nodded, he said, "When did you see Paul?"

"He was by here the other day." She pushed at her pale hair. "When you were riding range with Arguello."

"Why didn't you tell me?"

"I forgot about it till now."

He felt the back of his neck getting warm. "Paul and I were boys together. No reason to keep his visit a secret." He thought of what Hugo Ortlander had hinted at; some bloody business Paul was mixed up in at Mesilla. "Even if he has changed I'd like to see him."

"He'll be back. He's got a business proposition for you."

Chase swallowed the hard suspicion that lodged like a pebble in his throat. He found in her appearance a vent for his anger. She had worn the same green dress most of the week. And her hair was uncombed. He told her about it.

"When you get me the hired woman she can do the laundry," Marie said. "Then I'll always have a clean dress."

Chapter Five

PAUL DUBLIN and the old Cross Hammer crew finally arrived at Cross Hammer. The colonel's temper was becoming increasingly short because Dublin apparently had chosen to ignore his order to report here. One morning the colonel was finishing off a bottle of Pinchot's Reserve when he heard riders in the yard.

The sound alerted him. Benreed had taken the four old "pensioners" on a tour of the east range. The colonel was here alone. He picked up a rifle and levered in a shell as the riders swung across the yard. His mouth didn't pale from fear necessarily, but from anger. Whenever someone appeared suddenly as these riders had done, there was always the possibility they were Mexican. The colonel hated all members of that race, not particularly because they were Mexican but because they were a symbol of the bloody fight he'd been forced to make in order to retain control of the ranch he had stolen from them.

"Them Arguellos soured Herrick against the whole race," his neighbors used to say before the war. "They should've tucked tail an' run, accordin' to the colonel."

The Arguellos had not run. They fought. But at last Herrick and his men had forced those few left alive to quit the country.

So today when riders came swinging around the barn and into the yard, Colonel Herrick was ready.

But when he saw a boyish smile on the tough young face of the leader of the ten men who approached, he shouted, "Paul! Paul, my boy!"

Paul Dublin slipped from the saddle. He stood beside his horse. The other men swung down. The colonel nodded to them. They were the remnants of his old crew.

The colonel extended his right hand. "Shake it, Paul. Don't stand on ceremony. The war's over. Shake your colonel's hand."

Paul Dublin clasped the hand. He was of medium height, slender. He whipped off his dusty brown hat. His hair was chestnut, long and curly. His face was unlined. At his belt he wore a revolver.

"Colonel, I ain't seen you since the Yanks caught us in the woods. I seen you shot, but I couldn't reach you."

The colonel looked him over with an approving eye. "You had me worried, boy. I heard some bad things about you from up around Mesilla way."

Before Dublin could reply Luke Benreed came riding in. "Howdy, Luke," Dublin said. "Them Yanks sure kicked the pea green outa us, didn't they?"

Benreed put out a large hand to shake. "If Jeff Davis had made the colonel a general, things would've been different."

"Reckon that's not the only place Jeff stubbed his toe," Paul Dublin said.

"Now, boys," the colonel put in, "don't go holdin' it

against Ol' Jeff. He wanted to promote me but I had political enemies in his cabinet. Come into the house, Paul."

The house didn't look much different than it had the first day Paul Dublin had come here. Still the cherrywood furniture, badly in need of polishing. The portrait of Marie's mother over the fireplace. The colonel filled two brandy glasses. His face was hard as he handed a glass to Dublin.

"I'm a little surprised at you," he said. "I consider you the same as my son. That means you're Marie's brother. I figured you'd look after her and keep her from doin' what I'd hate most." A vein in the center of the colonel's forehead began to throb. "Marryin' Chase Iverton!"

"They was already married by the time I got back from the war." Dublin spread his slender brown hands. "Nothin' I could do about it then."

"Like I wrote you, Paul, I've got a beef contract—"

"You aim to take Marie away from Chase, don't you?"

The colonel frowned at this interruption. "You think I'd stand by and let my girl live under the same roof with that turncoat?"

"Why you hate Chase the most? On account of him fightin' North? Or on account of his pa beatin' you that day at Midway."

The colonel reddened and put a hand to his right cheek where several small scars were visible. "No mind *why* I hate him." The colonel's black eyes studied the younger man's face. "You've seen Marie?"

"Yeah—I've seen her." Dublin drained his brandy glass, set it on a cherrywood sideboard. "How you figure to get Chase?"

"It's got to be done carefully. Marie is in love with him, unfortunately—"

"I wouldn't be too sure about that, Colonel."

"What's that supposed to mean?"

Dublin's brown eyes were yellow-flecked. He smiled. "I know Marie probably better'n anybody. I know how she feels."

"How would you handle him, then?"

"Move easy. Get him dead to rights. Hang him!"

The colonel slapped Dublin on the shoulder. "For a

minute there you had me worried. I was afraid the fact that you grew up together would make a difference—"

"What happens when she's free of Chase?"

"I'll see that she marries a good man." The colonel started to say more, then broke off. Something in Dublin's eye caught his attention. "You don't ever want to get yourself saddled with a woman, Paul. Be free and easy. A woman ruins a man."

"That so?"

"I want you to get the crew and start—"

"I'm not comin' back to work for you. The boys aren't comin' back."

The colonel had been lighting a cigar. His head jerked up. "You're foreman. Benreed will be segundo—"

"No."

The colonel stared at this man he had raised. Paul Dublin was eight years old when the colonel found him at a burned out wagon along the river. Paul was the only survivor of a Comanche attack.

"What's changed you, Paul?" the colonel said heavily.

"I fought a war for Texas. I aim to collect for it."

"That kind of thinking can get you on a sheriff's gallows," the colonel said crisply.

"I'll own me a good chunk of old May-hee-co before the fightin's over down there."

The colonel's black eyes narrowed. "You go mixing in the trouble down there and you'll wind up with your back to a 'dobe wall."

"Colonel, you recollect when them Yanks was maulin' us somethin' fierce how you told me that you knew where there was a thousand rifles an' ten thousand rounds of ammunition hid? That if them blue bellies pushed us back into Texas we'd git them rifles an' shoot the hell out 'em?"

The colonel brushed the back of a hand across his Imperial. "Do I understand you correctly?" The colonel's voice was ice. "You need weapons for this bloody business in Mexico?"

"Yep."

"You should know better than to suggest I'd have any part of a deal to arm Mexicans. Have you forgotten that I thoroughly hate every mother's son of them?"

"I could use them guns."

"If there are any weapons hidden in Texas, they're gone now." His mouth twisted. "Thanks to the Union Army of Occupation." He shot Dublin a sharp glance. "Is that the only reason you came here today?"

"If you got guns cached somewhere we'll make some money," Dublin said. "If you haven't—" The slender shoulders shrugged.

Dublin started for the door, but the colonel caught him by a shirt sleeve. "I was counting on you to come back with me, Paul."

"When the shootin's over down in Mexico maybe I'll come back one day ridin' in a Chihuahua coach full of gold."

The colonel wore his poker face when he stood in the yard and watched the men mount up. There was Elmo Task, the gunman, even shorter than Hugo Ortlander. There was Tom Bern and Sam Riondo and all the others. And now they were quitting him. Because of some blue chips they thought were theirs for the taking in Mexico.

If they thought he'd beg them to stay they were mistaken. The hell with them. But when they all rode out, Dublin in the lead, the colonel's mouth trembled. He went back inside and stood looking at the portrait of the woman he had married so long ago.

"You've put a curse on me," he said in a shaking voice. "You didn't give me a son. Now even Paul has turned his back on me."

That night the colonel told Benreed of the conversation with Dublin. He said that Benreed would have to line up a crew.

"So Dublin figures to keep Maximilian sittin' on his throne down yonder," Benreed said.

"I don't know which side he's fighting on. Maximilian's or that mestizo Benito Juárez. I don't give much of a damn."

"Reckon I'm foreman now, huh?" Benreed said.

"Temporarily, at least. Paul will come to his senses."

"I remember Dublin talkin' in the war. He claimed you never give him any pay when he worked here."

"He was like my own son," the colonel snapped. "You don't pay your own son a salary."

Benreed watched the bearded face. "Dublin claimed he went around with his bottom side hangin' out. That he didn't have no clothes to speak of. An' he always had the worst hoss in the string to ride—"

"I was trying to make a man of him. Toughen him up so he could run Cross Hammer when I'm gone."

"Dublin claims you done as bad to your own daughter. That you're poorly when it comes to spendin' money on anybody but yourself."

"You're getting on pretty dangerous ground with me, Luke," the colonel warned.

"I just want you to know if I'm foreman I figure to get paid. I want it in writin' so's when we get that herd to Kansas I get my share and no argument."

"Every man knows my word is my bond!" But when Benreed just looked at him, saying nothing, the colonel added, "I'm going to need a tough foreman, Luke. I'll draw up a contract with you."

This seemed to satisfy Benreed. But nothing would satisfy the colonel. That night he got drunk, locked up in the big house alone. The war, his wounds, his convalescence in the Yankee prison all had aged him.

The next morning Benreed looked at the colonel's bloodshot eyes, noted the sour whisky smell on his breath. "You have a bad night, Colonel?"

"A bad night living with myself."

"Get your daughter back and you won't be alone."

"That I'll do. I'm going to give Chase Iverton all the rope he needs. I want a good reason for hanging him. One my daughter will understand and accept."

He looked south, toward Mexico and thought of Paul Dublin. His mouth twitched. He went into the house.

Chapter Six

THE NEXT DAY Paul Dublin came by Flatiron. With him was Tom Bern, one of the former Cross Hammer riders and a veteran of the Confederate Army. He was a lank man with a ragged beard and greasy clothing. Bern hung back while Dublin came on ahead and sat his saddle looking down at Chase. The two men regarded each other quietly for a moment.

"I had a hoss shot out from under me at Shiloh," Dublin said. "You the billy boy that pulled the trigger?"

"If I was I'm glad it was only the horse I hit."

Dublin laughed suddenly and pumped Chase's hand. He was shorter than Chase. In addition to a belt gun there was a telltale bulge under his gray wool shirt that told of a hideout there. "You don't look a sight different," Dublin said, "than when we used to fish at the Fork." Dublin came close, winked. "Remember them Mex gals we had along the river?"

"Hold up on talk like that," Chase said with a faint smile. "I'm a married man now."

"You remember Tom Bern," Dublin said.

Chase nodded. Bern said "Howdy," and took the horses down to the barn.

Chase looked his old friend over. "I didn't quite know how you'd feel about me, Paul. The war and all. And me marrying Marie."

"Don't make no mind to me," Dublin said lightly. "One thing for sure, the colonel ain't very happy about it."

"For Marie's sake I hope he doesn't push me too far."

"He'll push, don't worry none about that. But he'll take his time about it." Dublin spat on the ground. "Don't reckon Marie will shed no tears if you have to kill him. She hates him powerful."

"Yes, I know."

Dublin was looking around at the mud-walled buildings of Flatiron. Here and there spring grass was growing out of sod roofs. "Flatiron don't look much different than it did when your pa was alive. It's good to see it again."

"You haven't seen it since the old days?" Chase said.

"Nope."

"Marie said you dropped by the other day."

Dublin was looking toward the barn, his back to Chase. Now Chase saw a stiffening of the slender body. Dublin turned, his boyish smile not quite reaching his eyes. "I figured she didn't want you to know, Chase. I—I, well, I figured it wouldn't look right. Me bein' here with you gone and all. It wasn't important anyhow."

"If it was as unimportant as you seem to think, there was no need to keep it a secret."

"I figured you might be jealous." Dublin's bright gaze rested on Chase. "Marie wants us to do business together. I didn't want to ruin it."

Chase picked at a broken thumbnail, remembering Dublin had always had the knack for talking himself out of an unpleasant situation.

When they walked to the house Chase noticed that Marie had put on a clean dress and brushed her hair and tied it with a ribbon.

"Hello, Paul," she said warmly. "I told Chase you were here the other day. I thought it best."

"You two are making something mysterious out of nothing at all," Chase said and felt his stiffened lips form a reluctant smile. "Let's say no more about it."

Marie smiled happily as the two men seated themselves at the scarred table. Chase poured drinks in two tin cups.

"It would be wonderful if you two could do business together," she said lightly. "But I leave that sort of discussion to the men. I'm going out and get some air and contemplate my sins."

"You got sins?" Dublin joshed. "That's one thing I got to see."

"You'd be surprised," she said, and her gaze quickly touched his face. She went outside, humming softly.

While Chase sipped his drink Dublin explained his business proposition. "I got a friend in Mexico who's goin' to have a good chunk of Chihuahua in his pocket. Or he damn soon will have when Maximilian buries Juárez."

"You're in for a bad fall," Chase warned, "if you plan to get rich by siding with the royalists."

Dublin bared his teeth. "I'm bettin' high that you're wrong, Chase. I'm bettin' my life."

"You can't bet higher than that."

"We're not goin' to lose." Dublin went on to talk about his friend in Mexico. The man's name was Mike Thorpe but because of slant eyes that gave him an oriental look the Mexicans called him *El Chino*. He owned a cattle ranch in the mountains which he called *Tres Caballos*. "He's a tough bird even if he does only have one leg."

"Where do I come in on this, Paul?"

"Chino needs hosses and guns."

"Revolution is a damned bloody business," Chase said firmly. "I want no part of it."

Dublin gave a significant look around the room with its mud walls, the dirt floor, the stove propped up on 'dobe bricks. "You oughta think of Marie. My kind of business pays big."

"You run guns to this Chino," Chase said slowly, "and it will give him more power than one man is entitled to. The result will be death for innocent people."

"Death is everybody's name in Mexico."

Chase shrugged. "The people down there have the right to work out their own problems without interference."

"Oh, hell, Chase, you sound like a Bible shouter. Sell your horses to Chino. Marie says—"

Chase stood up. "I've got a buyer. You and Bern staying for supper?"

While Chase cut steaks at the meat block Marie and Dublin talked about the old days at Cross Hammer. Marie wouldn't speak to Chase. He knew she was angered because of his refusal to throw in with Dublin. For some strange reason Chase had the feeling that Dublin didn't give much of a damn whether he joined him in this deal or not. He wondered just why Paul was acting this way.

When the steaks were frying Chase went to the door and shouted for Arguello and Bern to join them.

After supper Chase went down to the corrals to look over his horses. Arguello and Bern trailed along.

When he had gone Marie said, "Paul, why is he so stubborn? He could make money if he'd only try."

"He's not smart like me." Dublin grinned across the table at her. They were drinking a final cup of coffee. "I knew he wouldn't side me in this. He always did have the guts of a rabbit."

"You don't like him much," Marie accused.

Dublin said nothing. He sipped his coffee.

"Why do you want him as a partner if you don't like him?" she persisted.

"Maybe it gives me a chance to be around you." Dublin's eyes were wicked as he leaned across the table.

"I always wondered what Chase said the first night. Did he know he wasn't first through the hoop?"

She reddened and looked away. "Chase isn't exactly a fool. He never mentioned it."

"I'm like your pa, Marie. If you want somethin' bad enough it's not how you get it that's important. It's the gettin' that counts."

"You've spoiled my mood by mentioning Poppa."

"You hate him bad."

"He never wanted me." She looked down at her hands clenched on the edge of the table. "Now I don't want him."

"Maybe the colonel ain't glad he got a daughter. But I wouldn't pay you no mind if you was born a boy."

"Oh, stop it, Paul." She gave a nervous glance out the window to make sure Chase was still at the corral.

"I figured you'd wait for me," Dublin said.

"You could have written to me, you know." She regarded him. "Come to think of it I see no reason why I should have waited. You never once asked me to marry you."

"I figured we was courtin'. How else you think a fella courts?"

"You still never talked marriage."

He gave her his boyish grin. "You could've told your pa. I wouldn't have squealed too much if I was stood up to the preacher. With a shotgun nudgin' me."

"I bet you talked about us," she accused. "I know how men brag about such things."

Dublin finished his coffee and got up from the table. "I better go outside. I figure Chase is still some hotted up about me bein' here the other day. No use to get him steamin' for sure." He went to the door and looked back. "You remember what I said about wantin' somethin' so bad it makes no mind how you get it."

When Paul Dublin had gone outside Marie looked at the dishes in the pan that she would have to wash. The dirt sickened her. She sank to a chair and put her head on her arms that she crossed at the table edge. This talk with Paul today had upset her. It brought to mind all the ugliness of her life at Cross Hammer. Her father had gone away to fight a war when it wasn't necessary. Send-

ing her to a school in St. Louis so he could fight his war
without worry. And when the school was finally forced
to close because of hostilities she had come all the way
back to Texas by broken-down stage coach, and the last
hundred miles or so by mule back. Spending the rest of
the war years alone in the big house at Cross Hammer,
with only four old cowhands for companionship. If it
could be called that. Was this the depth of her hatred
for Josh Herrick, colonel in the forces of Jefferson
Davis? Or did this hatred go deeper.

And thinking of it now in this sorry house at Flatiron
she remembered where it started. The night her mother
was so sick and her father left the ranch for the Cross
Hammer horse camp. Because a dolt of a cowhand had
accidentally shot in the leg Robbie Boy, a stallion her
father hoped to race at Austin. And her father had gone
swiftly in the night, worried that the prize horse might
have to be destroyed.

During the night the condition of Marie's mother
grew worse. And two of the hands were put on fast
horses, one to ride for San Carlos and the doctor. The
other to fetch her father.

Her mother died an hour before Josh Herrick could
get home.

Marie was nine. And she remembered clearly seeing
her father swing off a mud-splattered horse and rush for
the house.

Marie said shrilly, "Momma's dead! But it doesn't matter as long as you could save Robbie Boy!"

"I'll kill the horse if that will make you happy," her
father said later. And he left for the horse camp to personally destroy the animal he had managed to save that
tragic night. But months later she learned that he had
lied about killing the horse. Robbie Boy won some
money for him at Austin. For this she hated him.

And now her father had come home from the dead,
so to speak. And when he ordered her to leave her husband and return to Cross Hammer it had given her
pleasure to refuse. Even though, after the first weeks
here at Flatiron, she would have given most anything to
get away.

Why was her life so complicated? she asked herself

as she stared through the window and saw Chase and Paul discussing something down by the barn.

And as she watched she weighed one man against the other.

Chapter Seven

AT SUNUP CHASE went down to the bunkhouse and roused Arguello and the two guests. The sun felt warm against his face. In the three corrals the horses were frisky with the coming day. There were some good things in the world after all, he thought. Last night he had not spoken to Marie. He knew it was childish in a way but it had irritated him that she would put on a clean dress and comb her hair for Paul Dublin. When she wouldn't do the same for her husband.

But he knew there was no use in bringing it up. She would have some excuse for her action as usual.

After breakfast Tom Bern said he reckoned he'd ride on. Dublin said he'd join him later.

Chase and Arguello pushed some of the horses to El Tigre Canyon a mile from Flatiron headquarters. By the time he returned the wind had come up. In looking back over the incident he supposed that this was what had drowned out sounds of his approach. He dismounted by the barn entrance. Wind devils whipped across the yard throwing bits of straw into the funnels of dust. Sand struck noisily against the barn wall.

He started for the house, wondering at the lack of activity there. Marie had said she was going to wash her hair and Dublin had claimed he would take a nap in the bunkhouse.

As he drew abreast of the west wall he saw them standing there out of the wind. Dublin stood with his back to Chase. Marie was facing him. At that moment her eyes, barely visible over Dublin's shoulder, widened with shock.

She began to scream, "No, Paul, no!" She suddenly clawed his right cheek.

For a moment Dublin stood foolishly. His cheek was bleeding. "What the hell—" But he did not finish it. For he saw Marie's stricken gaze and noted the direction in which she was looking.

The boyish smile replaced the foolish look on Dublin's face. As Chase started for him, Dublin backed up.

"Wait, Chase," Dublin said hoarsely. "You got to understand. I been in love with Marie since she was a kid. I done wrong. It won't happen again!"

Chase lunged for him and Marie screamed, "I hate you, Paul. I *hate* you!"

Chase closed quickly. The smile on Dublin's face became a snarl. Sidestepping the sobbing Marie he moved a hand toward his revolver. Before Dublin could grab his bone-handled belt gun Chase lashed out. His wild swing caught Dublin on the cheekbone. And the force of the blow knocked the shorter man against the barn wall.

With a low cry of pain Dublin again tried to reach his gun. Chase hit him again, knocking the gun loose. As Dublin bent to retrieve the weapon Chase met his face with an uppercut. The blow smashed Dublin's nose. He fell heavily to hands and knees.

With an oath Chase jerked him to his feet. He backhanded him across the face. As Dublin reeled away, Chase said, "Touch her again and I'll kill you!"

The two men glared at each other for a moment. Marie was sobbing, hands over her mouth. Taking Dublin by the arm Chase marched him to his horse. Dublin was bleeding all over the front of his shirt. Chase made him saddle up; but first he removed the man's rifle from its scabbard.

He forced Dublin to ride out, unarmed. "Don't come back!" Chase shouted.

Dublin, his face bleeding from scratches and smashed nose, shook his fist.

When he was gone Chase went to where Marie was huddled against the barn wall. "You seemed to get mad at him at just the moment I saw you together," he accused.

She was wiping her eyes on an unironed handkerchief. "You think I deliberately let him kiss me?"

"I don't know. I didn't see that much of it." He felt

frustrated and old and as foolish as Dublin had looked. What else could go wrong? he asked himself. Was this also part of the price he must pay for carrying a musket against his homeland?

He got his horse and spurred to a knoll and there fashioned and smoked five cigarettes. He was shaking. He looked down at the buildings of Flatiron, remembering his plans. He would sell the horses he had broken. And with money from this sale he would hire riders. No one in the Bend would work for him, that was sure. He'd been lucky to hire Miguel Arguello. In normal times he could hire a crew of vaqueros from across the line. But with the fighting down there most Mexicans were interested in the preservation of their homeland. They had no time for a Yanqui interested in the preservation of his rancho.

On this cold and windy spring day Chase felt his dreams were as strong as wet paper. The dream to get a crew—perhaps from New Mexico. Up there they weren't so particular which side you had fought on in the war. With this crew he would make his gather and perhaps before the year was out he could push a herd to the Kansas market.

He got into the saddle again and started down the slant for home. Home! The thought brought a twisting of his lips.

And then despite the happenings of this day he vowed not to be defeated. If they pushed him out of Texas he would be through for all time. And despite the hatred of his neighbors. Despite the treachery of Paul Dublin, he would fight.

When he got back to the house Marie rushed into his arms. "Oh, Chase, it was horrible. Horrible. I never want to see Paul again."

"You won't if I can help it."

She drew back, looking up at him, her blue eyes wide. "Honey, I know what you're thinking. But don't. I'll make it up to you. I'll make it up to you right now!" She held out her hands to him.

For a moment he stood looking at her, then he said, "You know how to fight a man."

"A woman's weapons—"

"There's a time and place for this," he said, and went

outside. He felt that today for the first time the victory was his.

And if this angered her she did not show it that night in the quiet of the mud-walled house.

For the next several days there were nagging little incidents that put a further strain on him. Somebody sneaked down one night and unlatched a corral gate and some of the horses got loose. It took several hours the following day to round them up. Then a rifleman from the knoll behind the house creased one of the horses, a bay, knocking it unconscious. The shot could as easily have killed it had there been the slightest miscalculation. In a rage Chase pursued the rifleman, but lost the trail along the river. He never did get a good look at the assailant.

He lost sleep and the slightest sound brought him out of the house, rifle in hand, no matter what the hour. Miguel Arguello shared in this; twice he was fired on.

Once when Chase was trying to make a rough tally of cows in his Flatiron brand, he was caught in a crossfire that kept him pinned behind a boulder for most of one afternoon. His horse had wandered off and it took an hour's hike in high-heeled boots to run him down.

Nagging little things that pulled at a man's nerves and put his temper dangerously near the exploding point.

"Paul's behind this," he told Marie. "I'll bet my last dollar on it."

"If we don't sell those horses we'll be down to our last dollar," Marie said. "Chase, why don't you make it up with Paul?"

"No."

"He's just like a brother to me. He meant no harm that day."

"Then why did you claw his face?"

"He surprised me so. I can handle him. Throw in with him, honey. Sell your horses to this Chino. We can live like *ricos* in Chihuahua once the fighting is over."

He gave her a suspicious look. "That sounds like Paul. Did he put those words in your mouth?"

Two days later he saw buzzards wheeling in the sky some distance from the house. When he rode over to investigate he saw that one of his cows had been knifed. Knifed so a shot wouldn't arouse the occupants of the house. Choice parts of the beef had been carried away, the rest left for the buzzards. The thief had brazenly left his sign. Lying beside the butchered beef was the hide with its Flatiron brand. Most range tramps slow-elking a beef would at least bury the hide. Chase felt a surge of anger. Whoever had done this didn't give a damn whether they were caught or not.

He knew it was foolhardy to follow the tracks of a single horse that led away from the dead cow. But he'd had enough. It was time somebody was taught a lesson. The tracks might lead him into a trap and if they did he'd worry about it when and if it happened.

The trail led toward the river, twisting through hills. At last through willows he saw the Rio. He also saw shacks made of willow poles, and a corral. Once before the war this had been a rustler hangout. There were two horses in the corrals, two Mexican saddles with oversize horns straddled the top pole of the corral fence.

Chase felt a prickly sensation at the back of his neck. He swung down, a shell under the hammer of his rifle. This could be a fool play, he told himself. Risking your neck for one dead cow.

The door to the nearest shack opened suddenly. A dark-haired girl stepped out, a carbine under her arm. So surprising was her appearance that he stood for a moment with his mouth open. Down on the river in an old rustler hangout you didn't expect to find a black-haired girl, tall, slender, with regal carriage. She should wear a mantilla and have a high Spanish comb in her hair and be riding the streets of Chihuahua City in an Imperial coach. You discounted her man's wool shirt cinched in at the waist by a wide leather belt. The tight-fitting black breeches, the boots. It was her face, the way she held herself that made you realize that here was quality.

He took a few steps forward, then halted.

She said in a low voice, "What do you want?"

He found his voice, telling her about the butchered cow. About the tracks that led here.

"I know nothing about this," she said. "We just arrived."

"We?"

"My brother and I. He's inside. He has a rifle trained on you through the window. Don't do anything foolish."

"Why doesn't he come himself to face up to a man?" Chase said thinly. "Instead of sending his sister?"

She just looked at him. Now he could see that she wasn't Spanish as he had at first supposed. Her eyes were blue, not light like Marie's, but dark. Even in man's clothing there was a handsomeness about her, for she curved in a woman's way at bosom and hip.

A harsh voice came from the shack. "Tell him to come in, Jessie. I want to look him over."

Her dark brows lifted and she shot a glance at the shack. "Let him go," she said. "We have enough trouble without adding to it."

"Get him in here! Or I'll shoot his goddam legs from under him."

Her shoulders shrugged under the gray wool shirt. "You'll have to forgive my brother," she told Chase. "These are very trying times. He's suspicious of everyone."

Chase hesitated. Ahead and a little to the left was a large rock. He could chance the rifle fire of the man inside and take shelter there. But the girl might be hurt in the exchange of fire. He decided to gamble.

He gestured for the girl to go in first, then he followed. A shaggy-haired man was seated behind a long table. He held a revolver pointed at Chase. His face was round, his nose a turned-up stub of flesh. The most arresting thing about him were his eyes. They were long and slanted, giving him an oriental look.

A name leaped into Chase's mind: "El Chino," Chase said aloud.

"Where'd you hear about me?" he demanded.

"Paul Dublin."

The man lowered the gun slightly. "You know Dublin?" Chase nodded. "My name's Iverton."

"I never heard Paul mention your name." Chino looked at his sister. "How about you, Jessie?"

"I remember. This man Iverton married Paul's old sweetheart. Paul got drunk last time he was down at *Tres Caballos*. He told me about it."

"Just what did he tell you?" Chase asked.

She put her carbine on the table. "How would you feel toward the man who married your girl?"

Chase stood with the rifle under his arm, his eyes thoughtful. So Paul hated him for marrying Marie. Then why that pretense of friendship, brief though it was?

"I guess he also told you," Chase said, "that I fought for the Union."

He was looking at the girl, but her brother answered. "We've got our own war in Mexico, Iverton. We never worried much about yours."

"You're supporting Maximilian," Chase accused.

"I support the side that figures to win. Juárez won't last six months."

"I have a feeling you're wrong."

The slanted eyes appraised the tall, brown-faced Texan who had come in search of the butchers of his cow. "Talk like that would get you stood up against a 'dobe wall. If you were south of the line."

"But I'm not south of the line," Chase reminded. He looked around the room. Six bunks were built against the walls. On the floor were saddles, ropes, old boots and other gear. Beside a rear door was a rusted stove. Not much worse than my own home, Chase thought bitterly.

Chino said, "You mentioned something about a butchered cow. There's leavings out back." He jerked a thumb toward the yard.

"Somebody ate well last night," Chase said thinly. "Likely Paul Dublin."

"We're waiting here for him to come back. Wait with us. You can ask him yourself."

And with this Chino started to pick up the revolver again. Chase had been anticipating this move. Quickly he caught the gun with the back of his hand. Before Chino could tighten his grip on it, Chase sent the revolver skating across the table and to the floor.

Chino regarded him darkly. "I should've blown you in two when I had the chance."

"Oh, stop it," Jessie said impatiently. Her blue eyes slanted to Chase. "You've got a chance to get out. Take it."

He stared at her, wondering at her connection with a pack of ruffians like the crew Dublin ran with. There was strength on her handsome face, also a weariness.

Her mouth was full, red against her face that was lightly colored from the sun.

Suddenly Chino got to his feet and leaned across the table. He made a futile attempt to grab Chase by the arm. When Chase drew back his fist, Jessie said, "Don't fight him. He's a cripple."

"I can fight with one leg as well as two!" Chino cried at his sister.

As if to prove it he hobbled around the end of the table and lashed out at Chase. But Chase was staring at the stump of right leg. For the first time he saw the crude crutch on the floor near Chino's chair.

In this moment when he looked away Chino's fist struck him in the face. Stung, Chase lashed out instinctively. His fist crashing against Chino's jaw knocked the man off balance. Chino hopped a few steps on his left foot, trying to regain his balance. But he lost it and fell heavily.

Chase went over and put out a hand to help him to his feet. But Chino ignored the hand. Clutching a corner of the table, he used it as leverage to pull himself erect. Jessie was frowning. She handed her brother his crutch.

"I'm not proud of hitting him," Chase told her.

"I guess he had it coming." She flashed her brother a cold look. She walked over and picked up the revolver that had been knocked to the floor.

"I'll walk with you to your horse," she said. "I don't think there's another weapon in this room. But if there is I doubt if my brother would risk trying to shoot you in the back. Not when there was a chance he might hit me accidentally."

"You're mixing in a deal that's none of your business, Jessie," Chino said.

"If this is none of my business, why did you insist I come along?" she flashed at him.

"Because it's not safe for you at *Tres Caballos*."

Chase walked with her out into the bright sunlight. Under one arm she carried her carbine. She had put her brother's revolver into the waistband of her black breeches.

"Do you like what your brother is doing in Mexico?" Chase asked.

She shrugged. "In times like these who knows what is

right?" She took a few more steps with her easy stride, then added, "No, I don't like what he's doing. But he's the only family I have. He needs me."

Just as he neared his horse there was the sound of riders moving up through the river sand. Quickly Chase pushed the girl behind him. He drew back the heavy hammer of his rifle.

He saw Paul Dublin and Tom Bern ride out of the willows thirty yards away. They drew up, surprise touching their tight faces. But they quickly recovered.

"You lookin' for somebody, old friend?" Dublin sneered. "Howdy, Jessie."

She did not reply to the greeting. The scratches on Dublin's face were livid. There was a swelling on his jaw and his nose looked almost as big as a sausage.

"Somebody's been slow-elking my beef," Chase said. He told them about the butchered cow and the tracks he had followed here.

Dublin seemed to think it was funny, as Chase knew he would. He wished mightily that Jessie were not present.

Dublin looked at Bern with the greasy beard. "We had some mighty prime steaks last night, Tom. Where'd you get that beef you brung in?"

Bern gave Chase a sly look. "I figured Flatiron cows was for the takin'. I heard the owner run off to Illinois or somewheres."

"You heard wrong," Chase said crisply. "Paul, this is your warning. Stay off Flatiron. I mean it!"

Chase backed to his horse. He drew his revolver and then booted his rifle. Holding the revolver so as to keep the two riders covered, he got into the saddle.

"Adios," Chase said to the girl, and touched the brim of his hat.

As he rode off he turned, getting a final glimpse of Jessie standing tall, her boots anchored in the sand. The sun was touching her dark hair.

What sort of girl rode with men like these? was the thought that persisted in his mind. As he sent his roan crashing through the willows a shot whipped the air overhead, giving off a sound like tearing canvas. And Jessie's strident voice: "Leave him alone, Dublin! I mean that!"

That night he could not sleep for he kept remembering Jessie Thorpe and how she had looked down there on the river.

And mingled with the thoughts of Jessie was a voice that hammered at him: Fool, fool. You made your brag to Dublin, ordering him to stay off Flatiron. And just how do you propose to enforce that warning, Chase Iverton? You have one hired hand. Could the two of you fight off Dublin and his crew if they chose to attack? Could you even think of standing up against the men Colonel Josh Herrick might send to crush Flatiron?

Maybe he should abandon Flatiron as his father had done before the war. Take Marie out of Texas.

But the thought was dead in him almost as soon as it was voiced. No, he'd stay and fight. And maybe if he died here someone would remember to put on his tombstone: Here Lies Chase Iverton, A Stubborn Man.

Chapter Eight

THE MEETING of Bend ranchers at Midway Store, called by Colonel Josh Herrick brought an air of expectancy to the rangeland. The news that the colonel possessed a Yankee beef contract had been the topic of conversation for a week or more. There was a slight hope showing on the faces of the shirttail ranchers like Ed Bates.

It had been agreed beforehand by Bates and Dave Franklin, that nothing—absolutely nothing was to be said about the attempted tar and feather incident at Midway Store. If the colonel had even a vague suspicion that his daughter was to have been a target along with her husband there was no telling what the result would be. Likely somebody would be dropped off the back of a horse on the end of a taut rope.

There was a good crowd in Ortlander's Midway Store this day. The corners of Ortlander's mouth were still raw from the gag the colonel had placed there not too long ago. Ortlander set out a bottle of the colonel's favorite whisky, Pinchot's Reserve.

"How do things look up Kansas way, Colonel?" a man said tentatively.

"Cow business is shaping up fine," the colonel said in a matter-of-fact voice.

When he did not enlarge on this Ed Bates looked around at the others, then said, "We're hoping you can spread that business around a little, Colonel."

The men awaited the answer breathlessly. So much depended on it. Against the wall sat Bart Coleman, the Bates foreman. His right arm was in a sling. It was doubtful, the doctor in San Carlos had said, whether he would ever regain the full use of his right hand.

Luke Benreed, foreman of Cross Hammer, lounged against the end of the bar, his gaze thoughtful. He had his hat tipped far over on the right side. On the left temple was an unhealed gash where the barrel of Chase Iverton's revolver had struck him down in a room upstairs.

The colonel enjoyed watching his neighbors sweat it out while they waited for his reply. He had his drink, then looked around at the men who were counting on his generosity to make them solvent at last. "I'm forming a pool for a Kansas drive," the colonel said. "Each man furnishes his own crew. I cut out twenty per cent of your herd for my fee."

"Your fee for what?" Hugo Ortlander said into the silence.

The colonel gave the little man a look of impatience. "I'm the one has the contract. It should be worth a lot for the boys to have a ready market."

Some of the ranchers looked angry, others worried. "Twenty per cent seems a bit high, Colonel," Ed Bates said and forked stubby fingers through his gray hair.

The colonel gave them all a patient smile. "You've got nothing now. Twenty per cent of nothing is still nothing. But if you go in with me—" He spread wide his hands. "I furnish the market. You boys furnish some of the beef."

Dave Franklin pushed through the crowd. "If we all go to Kansas it'll be a passel of beef. Just how many cows can them Yankees buy anyhow?"

"They mentioned ten thousand head."

There was a startled exclamation from the men. One of them gave a slow whistle. They looked around at each other. Ten thousand head of beef. And through their minds raced thoughts of what they could do with their share of the beef money.

Life began to flow into the grim faces of these men who had hung on here for so long.

"Buy the colonel a drink!" somebody shouted. "We'll all buy him a drink!"

"Hooray for the colonel!"

Colonel Josh Herrick lifted high his glass. "To Jeff Davis!" And there followed a strident rebel yell.

The adulation the colonel received in his store plainly nettled Hugo Ortlander. For a moment he forgot his stated neutrality. The men were crowding around, putting their names down on a paper the colonel had produced.

"You figure to cut Chase Iverton in on this deal?" Ortlander asked innocently.

There was a hushed silence. Ed Bates gave Ortlander an angry look. "That was a fool thing to say!"

"How long since you smelled stewed chicken, Ed?" Ortlander said levelly.

And Bates turned red and flashed a look at Franklin.

If the colonel noticed any of this he gave no sign. "Iverton is a turncoat," he said. "He deserves no consideration."

"He's your son-in-law," Ortlander reminded. "You boys oughta forget about the war. Give him a chance."

"He won't be my son-in-law for long," the colonel said, his scarred face pale above his beard.

"You aim to kill him?"

The colonel's gaze was bleak. "Marie will be home to Cross Hammer one of these days."

One of the men said, "I got no use for a turncoat, but you got to admit Iverton is long on guts tryin' to make a life for himself here."

The colonel wheeled, trying to spot the man who had spoken. But the crowd was milling around the bar and he couldn't see who it was.

The signatures were all on the paper, together with some Xs for those who could not sign their names. Eleven ranchers had joined the colonel's pool.

"I'm starting roundup tomorrow," the colonel said in his military voice. "You boys work your own range. In about two weeks push everything to my camp at Dutchman Flats. That'll be our holding grounds. We ought to be ready to move north in three weeks."

Dave Franklin gave the colonel a thoughtful look. "We get a big gather an' we'll be prime target for rustlers."

Sid Coames, a gaunt, red-eyed rancher, said, "I been worryin' about that too, Dave."

"It's a chance we'll have to take," the colonel snapped. Then he gave Coames a long look. "You got something on your mind?"

"Some of us boys been losin' hosses. I followed tracks. They lead to that old rustler hangout on the river. I figure before we start roundup we oughta clean the place out."

While the colonel rubbed his beard as if in deep thought, Ed Bates said, "I know the place you mean, Coames. That's where Paul Dublin's been hangin' out—"

His voice trailed off. There was an uncomfortable silence. Bates looked around, his gaze stricken. The colonel was regarding him strangely.

"I only meant," Bates floundered, "that if Dublin's in the rustling . . . I mean— What I mean is that Dublin won't hit any herd we gather. He's like a son to the colonel. Ain't that right, Colonel?"

A faint sickness touched the colonel's dark eyes, then was quickly gone. "Paul's a little wild. A lot of boys are these days. The war unsettled a lot of us. I'll ride down and have a talk with him."

"You'll have to do more'n talk," Ortlander put in across his bar. "From what I hear the law's after him for some shootings up at Mesilla."

"One thing to remember," the colonel said, looking around. "We've got no law here. None but our own. As head of the pool, I think it is my place to decide what if any action is to be taken in any matter whatsoever." He let that sink in, then bought drinks for the house.

Two days later the colonel left his roundup camp and rode south. The news that Paul Dublin had a hangout along the river had already been brought to his attention by Luke Benreed. The foreman had run into Paul down there. He had taken supper with Paul and his men.

For some unaccountable reason the colonel altered his direction so he would go by Flatiron. There was no logic to this, he knew. But perhaps he could end this bitterness that was eating at him like acid by facing up to Iverton with a gun. But he knew on second thought that this was foolhardy. Iverton had taken everything his neighbors had thrown at him. He was a tough man. You had to be a tough man, the colonel conceded, to come back where you were so despised.

Maybe at least he could see Marie. Iverton couldn't very well put a gun on the father who was on a visit to his daughter.

Some hours later he came to a knoll behind the buildings of Flatiron. For fifteen minutes he watched the place. There seemed to be no one about. At last he saw Marie come out of the house, a book or newspaper under her arm. She went to the shady side of the house where a chair had been placed. She sat down and began to read.

As the sounds of an approaching rider reached her Marie got swiftly to her feet and started for the house. Then she saw who it was. A copy of Harper's lay in the chair where she had been sitting.

"Hello, Poppa," she said in a dead voice.

He stood awkwardly by his horse. "Where's your husband?"

"Chase and Arguello went over to El Tigre Canyon to look at some horses."

"Arguello!" the colonel's mouth thinned. "You mean he's got one of *them* working here?"

"I don't like it much either, Poppa. But he's the only man who would work for Chase."

"Pack up your things— No, leave everything. I'll buy you new clothes. We'll leave before he gets back—" He saw that she was unmoved. She wore a blue dress he had bought for her before the war.

"You don't want to come home," he said finally.

"My home is here."

His face seemed to break apart. "All my plans for you. Can't you understand that everything I've done is for you?"

Her blue eyes were cold. "You went to war and left me."

"But I had to go. Our country was faced with invasion." The colonel's lips twisted. "Thanks to men like your husband."

"You didn't have to go to war, Poppa."

"I'll make it all up to you."

"The war wasn't the only time you deserted me, Poppa."

"I've never deserted you in my life."

"The night Momma died," she said, and turned into the house and closed the door.

She hates me, he thought bitterly as he rode away. She truly hates me.

Being at Flatiron today had revived all the old wounds. How long ago was it that the elder Iverton had fought him at Midway Store? Fifteen years at least. He remembered that day well. The place was full of his neighbors. He remembered Chase there that day, only a boy then, standing beside his father Ralph.

A drummer from Austin was in the store that day and he fawned over the colonel. After all, Cross Hammer had the potential of being the largest spread in the Bend.

"You've done right well in five years," the drummer told him.

Ralph Iverton said into the quiet that followed, "Yes, he's done right well, mister. Every section of land he claims title to was stolen from my friends the Arguellos."

The colonel felt a flush mount to his cheeks even now as he recalled that day. Remembered how he had called on Iverton to mind his own damned business. And Iverton, an older man by ten years or so, had shucked out of his brush jacket. He crossed the room with fists swinging. And the colonel had been forced to defend himself.

The fight had raged through the store and into the road. There was no mercy in Iverton. He had the strength of a river bull despite his years; and a sort of fanaticism that spurred him to perform the impossible. Colonel Herrick had always prided himself on being able to hold his own in a brawl. But that day he had been soundly whipped.

And now riding south toward the river he remembered the pain when Iverton repeatedly slugged him in the face, yelling, "Say it, Herrick! Say it!"

And at last Josh Herrick, half-unconscious from the beating, had said in a loud, clear voice, "I am a thief!"

If he lived to be a hundred and ten he would never forget the humiliation of that day.

For a moment the colonel was tempted to return to Flatiron and from a vantage point shoot down Chase Iverton when he rode in. But he knew, on second thought, that this would not do. When he finally disposed of this man he wanted a reason other than his hatred. He wanted Marie to know that the death of her husband was something that was above and beyond the bad feeling between son-in-law and father-in-law.

At the river the colonel found Dublin and the old Cross Hammer crew. Again he tried to talk Dublin into returning to Cross Hammer.

The colonel and Dublin walked down through the willows where the river flowed cool and green. "You still figure to get Marie a new husband?" Dublin said.

"Yes." The colonel looked at him. "Why?"

Dublin's gaze was hard. "I just wanted to hear you say it."

Colonel Herrick gave a small laugh. "We've been through this before, Paul. You and me aren't the marrying kind."

"You figure me for a son, you say." Dublin's voice was cold. "But I ain't good enough for Marie."

"We're different, Paul. We're cut from the same stuff. We've got no conscience. We take nothing from any man. That's why I like you, Paul. You're a hellion just like me."

Dublin broke off a willow twig, peeled the bark with a broken thumbnail. "A hellion you like. But not for Marie."

The colonel seemed not to hear. "I've got to get her out of Texas. She doesn't fit in here. You wouldn't want to be saddled with her. Believe me, she's just like her mother."

"If you care nothin' about her why do you give a hang whether she's married to Iverton or not?"

Mention of the hated name brought color to the colonel's face. "It's a matter of pride." The colonel touched his arm. "Come back with me, Paul. I'm begging you. It's something I've done to no other man."

"I got this big thing goin' in Mexico. I'm goin' to get rich. So goddam rich I can do anything I want."

"Let me warn you, Paul. Some of my neighbors are missing beef and horses. I've stuck up for you whenever your name is mentioned. You could end all this talk by coming home where you belong."

"You tell your neighbors to quit worryin' about me," Dublin said. "Chase Iverton's the one to do the worryin'."

"I don't want Marie hurt," the colonel warned. "That's why I haven't moved against him myself. One of these days if I wait long enough I'll have him in my sack."

"I was thinkin'," Dublin said, lifting a hand to the healed scratches on his face, "about them hosses Iverton figures to trail north."

"You steal from a turncoat," the colonel said, "and it isn't thievery at all. You understand, Paul?"

"I been hittin' at him a little at a time. He's goin' to get so damn sick of Texas he'll wish he never heard of it."

The colonel said, "Before I push the pool herd to Kansas, I'll come down and have another talk with you, Paul. Maybe you'll change your mind."

The colonel walked back to where he had left his horse by one of the shacks. Elmo Task held the animal for him. Task was way over forty, but still formidable with a gun.

The colonel said, "Elmo, if anything should happen to me, and Marie ever needs help—"

"You don't have to ask, Colonel," the little gunman said. "I worked for you a long spell. I was at Cross Hammer the night she was born. I think a heap of Marie. I'll watch out for her."

"Thanks, Elmo. I feel better hearing you say it."

When the colonel had gone, Paul Dublin called Bern aside. "Tom, we're pushin' south in two days. When I give you the word, grab some of Chase Iverton's hosses. An' push 'em north."

"North? I figure you'd want 'em for Chino—"

"Do what I say. I want Iverton away from Flatiron. Away from the river. Push them hosses hard. When you get into the Chalk Hills 'bush him."

"Why not kill him at Flatiron and be done with it?" Bern wanted to know.

"I got my reasons."

Joe Lombard, a big bluff man with a scar on his chin, rode in to report to Dublin. He said Dave Franklin and Ed Bates had around six hundred head of prime beef not more than four miles north, at a new roundup camp.

Paul Dublin smiled. "When we quit Texas, they're goin' to remember us a long time."

Several times that day he thought of the colonel and swore. "So he's goin' to find her a husband. But it ain't goin' to be me." Dublin clenched his fists and looked west and north in the direction of Flatiron. "We'll see."

Chapter Nine

CHASE TOLD MARIE that he was about ready to trail his horse herd to New Mexico. He planned for her to accompany him as far as Paso Del Norte. There she would wait for him until his return from the fort with money from the sale of the horses.

"It will be a holiday for you, Marie," he said.

The prospects of a journey seemed to please her. Her face became animated. She talked of what she would do in Paso while he and Arguello pushed the horses to Fort Ellenden.

That night after supper, when Arguello had gone to sleep in the bunkhouse, Marie said, "Who is Jessie?"

Chase looked up, knowing there was a startled look on his face. "Why do you ask?"

"You mentioned the name in your sleep last night. Is he a man you knew in the war?"

"Yeah. A man."

Later, rifle under his arm, he made a tour of his corrals. There was no suspicious sound. Nothing moved in the darkness. He went back to the bench before the house and resumed his wait. For weeks now he and Arguello had split up the night in two watches. At midnight Chase would relieve him. But when that hour came he felt no urge for sleep. He let Arguello have two more hours in his blankets.

Even when he at last went to bed Chase found sleep elusive. Since the day he had hit Paul Dublin there had been a strain between himself and Marie. He tried to relive in his mind the scene that day by the barn. How had they been standing when he came upon them so suddenly? Were Marie's arms about Paul's shoulders? Were their lips pressing together? Or had it happened as Marie said. Paul catching her by surprise. And she clawing him when the moment of shock was over.

He did not know how long he was asleep. Something awakened him. He jerked upright and swung his legs over the edge of the bed. It was pitch dark. He sat there a moment, while he cleared his mind of sleep.

He pulled on his pants. The sound that had awakened him came again. His horses were restless.

Then suddenly there was pounding of hoofs, a snorting of horses.

Snatching up his rifle he ran to the door and flung it open. "Miguel!" he cried. "Miguel!"

There was no answer, just a diminishing drum of hoofbeats heading east. Chase was rushing across the yard, clad only in pants and underwear. At first he thought all of his horses were gone. The corral nearest the house was full. The one beyond the stone breaking corral was empty.

He fired in the direction of the fading hoofbeats, knowing it was a wasted shot. A feeling of doom possessed him. He called Arguello's name again, urgently. He limped to the bunkhouse. Pebbles cut into his bare feet. He nearly stumbled over Arguello's body. The Mexican lay face down beside the overturned keg where he had been sitting.

At first Chase thought he was dead. Then he detected a slight pulse. He turned Arguello over on his back and struck a match. There was an ugly wound at the base of the man's skull. The wound was bleeding into the shirt collar. Arguello's breathing was ragged.

Shivering from the cold Chase struck another match.

He studied tracks on the ground. The assailant who had sneaked up behind Arguello had been wearing moccasins.

Comanches!

Chase licked dry lips, thinking of Marie alone in the house. Putting aside his rifle he carried Arguello into the bunkhouse. Marie was crying from the house, "Chase, what happened?"

He hurried to the house and dressed. He told Marie to build up the fire and heat water. He told her about the missing horses.

With a lantern he turned to the yard and studied the tracks. He had not told her about the moccasin prints because he didn't want to alarm her. A second look at the sign told him there had been only one man, riding a shod horse. The sign just didn't add up. Unless the Indian—if it was an Indian—rode a stolen white man's horse.

He had the feeling that the thief was a white man. A quick count told him there were eight head of horses missing. To the east a finger of gray appeared at the horizon. Making a swift decision he returned to the house. Marie had dressed. She gave him a long look out of her blue eyes. "Do you think Paul did this?" she asked.

"The idea occurred to me." Chase took down a shotgun from pegs above the door. He loaded the weapon and placed it on the table. "Use this if you have trouble," he said grimly.

"You're going after Paul," she said in a dead voice.

"I'm going after whoever stole those horses. Put a bandage on Arguello's head. He should be coming around soon."

She shivered. "I—I just can't stand the sight of blood."

"Don't lose your nerve," he said, gripping her by the arm. "You're a rancher's wife. Likely you'll see worse than this before your time runs out."

He went out into the growing dawn and looked in at Arguello. The man was beginning to stir. Because he could not take time to wait for the man to come around Chase saddled up. He rode out, rifle booted, brush jacket laced against the cold.

After two miles the tracks of the thief and the stolen horses veered sharply north. This was puzzling. The tracks were leading away from the river. Perhaps Paul Dublin wasn't responsible after all.

From the sign Chase knew the thief was driving the horses hard. He swore softly and thought, He'll ruin them if he keeps this up very long. But he knew he would eventually overtake them.

The trail led through brushy hills, across lava beds, then climbed through a rough canyon. He found two of his horses deep in the brush, their hides slick with sweat. They had broken away from the thief and he had not taken time to round them up.

He must know I'm after him, Chase thought.

The important thing now was to go after the rest of the horses and the man who had stolen them. These two could be picked up on the way back.

If he came back. The thought chilled him as he touched his roan with the spurs. There was more than an even chance that a man could die here in this lonely stretch of country and his body never found. He rode more cautiously now so as not to rush blindly into an ambush.

An hour later he saw a smudge of dust ahead. He showed his strong white teeth in a hard smile. Unless he was very much mistaken he'd be overhauling the thief within the next half hour.

After climbing a ridge he saw his horses in the distance. Ahead were the Chalk Hills. There were six horses milling around on the flats below.

He could see that a saddled horse was down. The saddler the thief had been riding. The thief was bending over the horse. It was a bay and its legs thrashed wildly. It tried to get up, making frantic sounds of pain. The right foreleg was strangely twisted.

The thief straightened up. He was turned sideways. Chase got a look at his face. It was Tom Bern with the greasy beard. The man who had come by that day with Paul.

Bern drew his revolver and put a bullet into the bay's head. The sound of the shot came rocketing up to where Chase sat his saddle on the ridge. The bay's legs were stilled. Bern holstered his gun and started stripping the saddle off the dead horse. When this was done he took his saddle rope and looked around for one of the horses. It was then that he saw Chase above him.

The distance was great for accurate pistol shooting, but Bern made his try. As the bullet fell harmlessly away, Chase swung down, rifle in hand. Bern lunged for his own saddle and his rifle in a scabbard. Just as he drew the weapon free Chase fired. The shot went winging between saddle and man as Bern threw himself aside.

Before Bern could swing up his rifle Chase cut loose with another shot. Bern fell as if hit with a mallet. He moved a few times on the ground.

Chase rode down cautiously. The sound of the shots had panicked his horses. They were scattering across the flats.

Chase dismounted some distance from Bern. He approached with revolver drawn. The sun was climbing. It was very hot. Already flies had matted the wound in the bay's head. Bern lay on his side.

As Chase approached Bern suddenly whipped over on his back. In that moment Chase saw the wound high up on the collarbone. He saw the blood and the bone itself. He saw Bern's lips white against yellowed teeth. The gun in Bern's hand spat a lance of orange flame just as Chase fired. Bern fell back, the gun slipping from his fingers.

Chase kicked the man's gun out of reach. He sat down on his heels. Now that it was over he felt shaky and gripped by a vast weariness. Bern's eyes were open. His two hands were pressed to his chest where the second bullet had entered. There was not much bleeding.

"Why one man?" Chase said. "Why didn't Paul send the whole bunch?"

"I damn near made it, Iverton. Yonder is the Chalk Hills. Guess my luck run short today. Got a drink?"

Chase shook his head. "Not even a canteen. I left in sort of a hurry, remember."

"Yeah." Bern grimaced with pain. "That Mex you got workin' at Flatiron has got a hard head. I had to hit him twice."

"A sneak trick wearing moccasins to come up on a man."

"No matter now," Bern said in a voice rapidly growing weaker. "Reckon I'm done, huh?"

"I'm going to rope one of my horses. I'll try to get you to San Carlos and the doctor."

"I ain't got twenty breaths left in me. We both know it."

Chase said, "Why were you heading north instead of to the place on the river?"

Bern gave a gusty sigh and his body went limp. Chase looked at the man for a long moment. Bern would never answer any questions again. He was dead.

Chase started to turn. A voice angled in from behind. "Just stand there, Iverton or I'll bust your back with a bullet. Charlie, go see who that is on the ground there."

The voice was vaguely familiar. Chase turned his head, saw that the man who had spoken was Max Coleman, foreman for the Bates 66 spread. Coleman still wore a bandage on his right wrist. He carried a revolver in his left hand. There were three men with him. They had been present that day at Midway Store.

The one called Charlie came up from the rocks where the men were partially concealed some distance away. Charlie had a round face, high cheekbones and a smudge of black whiskers on his chin. He peered down at the dead man.

"Tom Bern," Charlie said.

Coleman came up with the other two. He turned his stocky body and surveyed Chase with dark and angry eyes. "That bullet you put in my wrist, Iverton. I ain't forgot. The doc says my wrist will likely be stiff from here on out."

Chase stood with hands half lifted under the threat of Coleman's gun. It wouldn't take much prodding on his part for Coleman to shoot him down. Coleman was conversing with his companions in a low voice.

He gave Chase a hard grin. "The colonel's been itchin' for an excuse to get you in the bucket. He might pay fancy for knowin' what you done."

"I never said I shot Bern," Chase put in quickly. A shaft of fear touched him. He had never considered the possibility that the colonel might get in on this.

"We watched you from the ridge yonder." Coleman waved a hand behind him. "We're workin' roundup hereabouts. Camp is about ten miles east. Get his gun, Charlie."

Chase backed up a step. "You're not taking me to the colonel," he said hoarsely and tried to reach for his revolver.

But two of them came at him from behind and pinned his arms. Before they could bear him to the ground, however, he twisted free. But only for a moment. One of them climbed his back. The other one struck him in the face. This man he pitched to the ground near Bern's body. He flung the second one over his shoulders. Desperately Chase tried to grab his gun. But the weapon had slipped from its holster during the skirmish. He made a frantic lunge for Bern's gun that lay on the ground. He fell, rolling. He was inches short of the butt. When he tried to regain his feet, one of them got him around the knees, spilling him. They pinned him flat, face down. One of them landed with a knee in the middle of his back, driving the wind out of him.

When they finally yanked him erect his wrists were tied behind his back. They got him into the saddle of his roan. He kicked at them but at last they got his ankles roped under the horse's belly. One of them rode down a Flatiron horse. They saddled the animal then with a catch rope lashed on the body of Tom Bern.

For the first mile or so Chase argued with Coleman. What had the colonel ever done for him? he demanded. There was hardly a man in the Bend who didn't secretly hate Colonel Josh Herrick.

"I don't give a damn about the colonel," Coleman finally flung at him. "You ruined my wrist. I aim to see you pay for it."

"You drew on me, Coleman. I shot you to save my life."

Coleman said nothing to this.

It was some hours later when they reached the colonel's Cross Hammer roundup camp. Beyond the chuckwagon a sizeable herd had been gathered, held by some half dozen riders. The men were standing up in their stirrups to see who was riding in.

Colonel Josh Herrick was in earnest discussion with his foreman, Luke Benreed. It was Benreed who saw Chase and his escort first. He nudged the colonel.

The colonel looked around, saw Chase, saw the dead man. The colonel's shoulders straightened.

"I had a feeling about this day, Luke," he said, a gleam of triumph in his eyes. "A real feeling."

Chapter Ten

THE MEN GATHERED around the body of Tom Bern. You might have thought it was Jeff Davis himself laid out there under the harsh Texas sun. The colonel was eulogizing:

"Tom Bern fought under me in the war. A fine CSA cavalryman dead by a traitor's hand."

Chase, sitting on a shelf of ground, hands tied behind his back, cried, "He was a horse thief!"

The colonel turned and deliberately looked at a lone cottonwood tree with one sturdy limb, growing out of the side of a hill some thirty yards away. Then he put his black gaze on the prisoner. "You're going to have a long time to consider your sins, Iverton. A good long time!" A fierce smile stretched the bearded mouth. "You hang at midnight!"

The colonel sent riders to the other roundup camps, where they were to inform the pool members that they were needed at the Cross Hammer holding grounds. They were to leave only a minimum crew at the various camps. The rest were to come here. The colonel wanted a good-sized audience for what he planned. It would help erase an old humiliation perpetrated by the father of this man he intended to hang.

All afternoon there were the shouts, the popping of rope ends on hides. Branding fires gave off their smoke and stench. There was the frantic business of roping calves, dragging them to the fire. The application of cherry-red irons. But there was a system here, despite the seeming lack of direction. Each man knew his job. They worked with precision. They burned their hands on ropes, they wore out horses and switched saddles to fresh mounts.

The pool members began to arrive with as many men as they could spare from guarding the herds. Bates and Dave Franklin arrived last.

When Bates came to survey the prisoner, who sat on a shelving of rock, there was mixed emotion on the old face. A sort of triumph and at the same time sadness.

"You better help me, Ed," Chase said through his teeth. "Or I'll tell what you planned for Marie at Midway Store. The colonel would likely use his rope on you and Dave if he knew you figured to use tar and feathers on Marie."

A faint worry touched Bates, then he said, "Tell him if you're a mind. He wouldn't believe a turncoat."

Chase took a deep breath, held it a moment. He knew Bates spoke the truth. "At least send some of your boys to Flatiron. Marie's there alone—"

Bates gave Chase a worried look, then glanced at the colonel who was directing operations at the branding fires. "The colonel is running the show," he said stubbornly.

Bates walked away into dust clouds that lifted as a new bunch of cows was pushed down to the holding grounds.

All this time Chase sat on the rock near the chuckwagon. He seemed detached from all this, as if he might be observing a Texas roundup camp for the first time. These were men he had never seen before, men who did not even know that he existed.

Lacking this afternoon was any hilarity on the part of the men. They worked soberly. Those pulled in from the various pool roundup camps, took their leisure and occasionally glanced at Chase. There were maybe twenty men in camp.

In one way the afternoon was the longest he had ever spent in his life. In another way it seemed that the hours passed with terrible swiftness. The western edge of the sky flamed for a time and then became purple. A star glittered against a crimson cloud.

At the colonel's order Chase was untied and allowed to eat a plate of beef and beans. He had little appetite;

it seemed that his stomach was a cold knot of flesh. But
he drank the coffee that Ed Bates gave him. There was
a hangdog look in the old man's eyes. Bates took a
bottle from the pocket of his patched canvas pants and
poured a liberal shot into the cup that Chase held.

"Thanks, Ed," Chase said.

Without a backward glance Bates shuffled off into the
early darkness. Chase thoughtfully let his gaze slip to
the right where a man stood guarding him. To the left
was another man. This one was nearer. Chase turned
slowly, carefully so as to avoid suspicion from his guards.
The cowhands were scattered about the area, eating,
some with backs to rocks or wagon wheels. Others
guarding the herd would take their evening meal later.
Campfires blazed throwing a yellow glow across the
roundup camp.

The nearest guard stood with rifle under his arm. He
was squat, bearded, a man Chase did not know. Chase
looked past the man and tried to make his voice sound
startled as he said, "What the hell—"

The man followed the direction of Chase's glance.
Lunging forward Chase tried to snatch his belt gun. At
the same moment he dashed the contents of his tin cup
into the guard's face. The man screamed, fell back. The
tips of Chase's fingers brushed the butt of the man's
holstered gun. He made another grab. By this time the
camp was aroused. Somebody tripped him. He fell head-
long, rolled. A man shouted. Knowing his very life depended on getting away, Chase reared up. A thick arm
caught him around the neck with crushing force. Two
of them got him by the legs. With a final desperate surg-
ing of his body he tried to throw them off. But others
were coming in. They got his wrists and forced his arms
behind his back. This time the ropes cut off all circulation. They hauled him over to the rock where he had sat
for so long. They pushed him down.

The man who had taken the coffee and whisky in the
face was cursing. When he tried to hit Chase the colonel
stopped him. Another man was dazedly rubbing the
point of his jaw where Chase had struck him with a knee.

The colonel smiled down at Chase, while the men
gathered around, ominously silent.

"Fight, Iverton," the colonel said. "I enjoy seeing you fight. Each time you lose you die a little. I want you to die a lot before this night is over."

Chase was gasping for breath. His ribs ached where one of them had kicked him. His shirt was torn. "Now that everyone is here," he said, trying to keep his voice level, "I demand a chance to tell my story."

"There's nothing for you to tell," the colonel told him. "The facts speak for themselves."

Chase looked at the shadowed faces. "I demand my right to be heard!"

"You've got no rights, turncoat!" the colonel cried.

Chase got to his feet. He glared at the colonel with hatred. "You're hoping I'll crawl."

"And you will!"

"Give me one good reason for this business tonight."

"I 'most died in that Yankee prison," Colonel Herrick said with a trembling mouth. "And I come home and find my daughter married to you!"

"You want to kill me because I married your daughter. Not because Tom Bern is dead."

The colonel pointed at the small scars on his face that were visible in the flickering firelight. "I hope each scar equals one minute that you strangle at the end of my rope."

"Boys, listen to me." Chase made his appeal, knowing it might be his last chance. "Tom Bern stole my horses. I went after him. He tried to fight and I killed him. He's one of Paul Dublin's men—"

There was a shifting of feet, a clearing of throats. Chase saw some of the men exchange glances, and he felt a slight hope. Very slight.

Sensing the trend of the thinking, the colonel said quickly, "Don't try to drag Dublin's name into this."

"He's turned bronc," Chase, said, "and you know it."

"No. Paul's—"

"He's wanted for killings in New Mexico. He's turned thief."

"Paul's a little wild," the colonel said. "Nothing more."

Chase saw Max Coleman standing beside his boss, Ed Bates. "Coleman," Chase said, "tell the truth. There were Flatiron horses loose where I killed Bern."

"I didn't see no horses."

"One of your boys roped a Flatiron horse. The one you used to bring in Bern's body."

"Only one horse," Coleman said. Firelight flickered redly in his eyes. He put his left hand significantly over his bandaged right wrist. "You were ridin' one horse, drivin' another. You came on Bern and the two of you had words. He didn't even have a chance to get his gun loose. You shot him twice."

"Liar!"

The colonel turned his head and gave Coleman a thin smile. "Thanks for telling the truth."

"You invented that story, Coleman!" Chase cried. "While you're at it, tell the colonel how I happened to shoot you in the wrist?"

Coleman smiled. "We figured to tar and feather this turncoat, Colonel. But he got the drop on us." His face darkened. "He shot me."

"You were going to strip my wife and do the same thing to her—"

"The colonel knows better than that," Coleman said and gave the colonel a long look.

"No woman ever had to fear such a thing in Texas," the colonel said stoutly. "Iverton, you can't gain sympathy by such a story."

Ed Bates had gone pale at the mention of the incident at Midway Store. Now that he saw nothing was going to come of it, a little color flowed back into his face. He touched his foreman on the arm. "Max, you sure Tom Bern got shot just like you told it?"

"I seen the whole shooting."

The colonel turned on Bates. "You doubting the word of your own foreman?"

Bates gave a slow shake of his gray head. "Not exactly, but—"

"Keep out of this, Ed," the colonel told Bates brusquely. Then looking around, "Luke, there's whisky in my wagon. Break out those bottles."

Luke Benreed started for the wagon. "Sure thing, Colonel."

Some of the men followed Benreed, anxious for a little hair of the Texas dog to take the chill from their bones. And this chill was produced not altogether by the harsh spring night. Some of it was due to the grim business planned for later this night. Turncoat or not the man to die was the son of one who had given most of them a boost at one time or another in the old days.

A few of the men crowded around Ed Bates. The old rancher voiced what was on some of their minds.

"We been losin' cows, hosses," Ed Bates said. "I told you the other day. I've seen Paul Dublin near those tracks. I've seen Tom Bern there."

"Doesn't mean a thing," the colonel snapped.

"Tell us your side of this, Chase," Ed Bates said quietly. "From the beginning."

Chase swallowed in a dry throat. The ropes had long since cut off any circulation in his arms. He told how he had been awakened by the sound of horses being driven away from Flatiron. He told how he had found Miguel Arguello unconscious. How he had tracked the thief and found it to be Tom Bern.

"Leaving your wife alone," the colonel accused, "just to go after a few head of horses."

"What in God's name would you have done under the circumstances!" Chase cried.

"In the first place I'd have given my wife a decent place to lay her head of a night. Instead of that wolf pen you call a ranch!"

Chase appealed to the others. "This hate he holds for me goes back to my father. I'm not the only Texan who fought for the Union."

There was a sudden silence. There was a restless shuffling of feet; somebody coughed.

Chase pressed on. "The old timers remember why you hate the name of Iverton. My father was an old man but he whipped you."

Somebody pushed a bottle into the colonel's hand. It was very quiet in camp, save for the low of cattle and the stomp of horses tied off beyond the fires. Embers from the six blazing fires drifted skyward, then burned out in the blackness above.

The colonel's face was livid. He turned to his foreman. "Luke, shut him up."

Benreed's towering figure threw a swift shadow across the ground. He hit Chase on the point of the jaw. Chase fell backwards off the rock. He lay face down in the dust and in a moment began to make strangling sounds. "Turn him over on his back," the colonel directed. "We don't want him to suffocate before we hang him."

"Let's get it over with," a man said nervously.

"He hangs at midnight," the colonel reminded, and removed a watch from his pocket and glanced at the face. "He's got four hours."

Chapter Eleven

Ed BATES CALLED some of his neighbors to one of the campfires. He told them he felt Coleman was lying, that the colonel had probably given him some money to tell his story.

Dave Franklin clenched his hard hands. "I got a wife and four youngsters to think about. If I don't make that Kansas drive with the colonel I might as well go into the brush an' forget to live."

Another neighbor said, "Seems like you're changin' your stripes awful damn quick, Ed. In one breath you claim you can't stand the sight of Chase Iverton, an' now—"

"I still don't cotton to a man who'd fight against Texas. But I also don't cotton to us bein' a party to the colonel takin' his hate out on him. 'Cause he married Marie. Damn it, boys, right is right. This is dead wrong."

His neighbors shook their heads and walked away into the shadows, leaving Bates alone. After a moment Bates hunted up the colonel, who was relating some war experiences to some of those who had stayed home during the hostilities.

"Colonel, I been doin' some thinkin'," Bates began.

"Good," Colonel Herrick said, giving the older man a sharp appraisal. "A little thinking is what we need most in Texas. We'll use our heads and beat the Yankees at their own game. Stick with me, Ed, and we'll all have a sizeable piece of money."

"Colonel, I think Max Coleman lied about how Bern got shot. I think you know he did."

The colonel had been sitting on a wagon tongue. Now he got slowly to his feet. Men crowded in, quiet now, watchful. The colonel lifted high a half-filled bottle of whisky. Firelight put a bright edge of color across his face. "Here's to us selling Texas beef in Kansas."

Some of the men gave a half-hearted "yip-yip!" to that. The colonel took a drink, passed the bottle to Bates.

"You'll be selling beef along with us, won't you, Ed?"

Ed Bates swallowed. He looked miserable. There was a heavy silence. One of the night herders was singing softly about a gal he had left in Monterrey.

At last Bates put out a hand, took the bottle and drank. Smiling, the colonel slapped him on the back. "I knew you were with us, Ed. With us all the way."

"Yeah. Reckon I got no choice," Bates said in a small voice. He cast a look at the prisoner who had regained consciousness and was watching him from across the clearing. Bates patted his stomach. "I feel poorly. Reckon I'll take a little ride."

"You do that, Ed," the colonel said.

"I'll go down to my camp and see how the boys are makin' out." Bates looked at Dave Franklin. "You goin' with me, Dave?"

Before Franklin could answer, the colonel cut in: "The rest of the boys aren't so weak in the gut, Ed. You go along now."

The colonel, an unlighted cigar clenched in his teeth, began to relate a bawdy story he'd heard while a prisoner of the Yankees.

Bates rode south into the thick Texas night. He wanted to put himself as far away from the Cross Hammer camp as possible.

Less than four hours until Chase Iverton was swung by the neck off the back of a horse. It was criminal, Bates told himself. Criminal to do that to a man just because you hated him. Not like tar and feathers. These things could be worn off in time. But hanging was permanent.

What could he do about it? Bates asked himself. Alone in times like these a small rancher had no chance. The pool offered a way out. It was the only way out. Ed Bates was in the same position as his neighbors. He was about at the end of his string.

It was a good three hour fast ride to the Bates-Franklin roundup camp near the border. As Bates neared the camp he had the feeling that cattle were running in the distance, reined in, listening. The sky was overcast, and there was the smell of rain in the air. Far to the south he saw a flicker of lightning. He shivered.

There was no mistake about cattle being on the move. The ground underfoot was shaking. There was a rumble, and it wasn't thunder. It was the smash of hoofs upon the ground some distance away. He felt dry in the throat and his heart strained unnaturally.

"Holy Mother," he breathed, and pushed on.

He came to a rise of ground. Lightning flashed and he saw cows on the run a hundred yards away. He could hear shouts and a gunshot now, flame making a jet of color against the darkness.

Down a long draw the cattle streamed. Away from the camp. South. South toward the river. As he neared he saw riders and thought, "Mex raiders from across the line."

But one of them was close by and Bates heard him curse. It was an English oath. "Goddam," the man said.

Bates drew his rifle and rode in. He saw the chuckwagon he had left earlier in the day when summoned by the colonel. It stood with its canvas top ghostly white against the black velvet night. The cattle were still moving swiftly, a quarter of a mile away.

A sudden dread gripped him as he thought of the men he had left here. Five? Six? He couldn't remember. When he saw a dark shape on the ground ahead, he swung down and struck a match. He looked into the dead face of one of his riders. He felt cold and his stomach turned.

A few feet away he saw another darker shadow. It was also a man. He struck a match. This was Flint Bishop, one of Dave Franklin's riders. He had been shot in the chest. But one side of his face had been crushed in, probably from the hoof of a horse or cow. Bates was sick upon the ground.

What was happening? was the thought that spun through his mind. What in God's name was happening?

And then he heard a horse approaching. He turned, peering into the darkness. He could make out the horse now, but no rider.

Then something caught him by the belt, in front, and jerked him up close. And his face was no more than four inches from another face.

Paul Dublin's voice said, "By damn, it's Ed Bates."

"You goddam thief!" Bates cried. "I tried to tell the colonel—"

"One of your boys claimed the colonel figures to hang Chase Iverton," Dublin said. "But he died on us before I could get the story straight. Chase dead yet?"

"You son of a bitch!" Bates screamed, and tried mightily to get free of Dublin so he could swing up his gun.

Dublin stepped back, firing his gun into the belt he had been holding a moment before. As Bates slumped, he shot him again.

Dublin rode to where a man said, "That you, Paul?"

"Yeah."

"Who was it with the matches?"

"Old man Bates. Good thing I went back. Keep those cows moving, boys!"

"They're movin' like Hell's door was at their backs."

"Let's get 'em across the river before this damn storm hits." Dublin threw back his head and cried, "*Viva El Chino!* Wait'll he sees the beef we got to feed his army!"

The herd had slowed now and Dublin rode to where Elmo Task was trying to force some of the cows into the river. Dublin drew the little gunman aside.

"You ride with me, Elmo," Dublin said. "We'll catch up with the rest of the boys later. I got a few things to pick up."

They headed east, paralleling the river for a mile or so, then cut north.

Chapter Twelve

CHASE WORKED his jaw. It was sore where Benreed had hit him. He sat on the rock, roped hand and foot. He heard the far-off cry of a coyote. He smelled the spring grass, the sharp odor of the whisky the men were drinking. He listened to the joshing. And he thought, They're going to kill me. They laugh while they wait to commit murder.

He closed his eyes and thought of Marie back at Flatiron. What would her life be now with him dead?"

. He saw the colonel remove his watch from a vest pocket and go over to one of the fires and use the light so he could read the figures on the watch face. The colonel smiled thinly, snapped the watch case shut and returned it to his pocket.

"One of you boys got a gentle horse?" he said. "One that'll stand for a spell with a roped man setting his back?"

"I got one," a man said.

"Pull his saddle," the colonel directed. "We'll set Iverton sideways on account of his tied ankles."

Chase saw a coil of rope sail over the limb of the cottonwood across the clearing. His heart sank into cold waves of fear that engulfed every fiber in his body.

One of the men led a gray horse under the cottonwood limb. He stripped off his saddle.

Most of the men were gathered by the tree. There was only a handful near the rock where Chase sat. He saw the colonel talking with Benreed. Then the colonel started walking toward the rock.

A man to Chase's right moved into his line of vision. The man wore a hat pulled low. A bulky blanket coat, the lashes hanging loose at the front, was slung over his shoulders. There was something about the way the man stood that caught Chase's attention. He tried to turn, to look closer at this man but at that moment the colonel came up.

The colonel bent low, hands on knees, cigar jutting from his lips. The tip of the cigar was only an inch from Chase's face.

"I've prayed for this moment, Iverton," he said tensely. "I've prayed hard for it."

"I'm not going to beg for my life. But think of Marie. You murder her husband and she'll never forgive you."

"I wonder." The colonel's eyes were very bright. He started to straighten up and then something caused him to look toward his left. Chase saw him flinch as if touched by some loathsome object. The colonel looked down. Chase followed his gaze.

The twin tubes of a shotgun, the barrels sawed short, projected from a blanket coat. One brown hand held the sawed-off shotgun. The other gripped the front of the colonel's shirt.

Chase lifted his gaze. The dark face under the low-pulled hat belonged to Miguel Arguello.

The colonel seemed frozen in that half crouched position. His mouth hung open. Those nearby saw that something was wrong. One of the men started forward.

The colonel said, "Wait. Hold it!" His voice was shaking.

Miguel Arguello said firmly, "Do not even breathe too deep, Senor. Or my finger may slip off these shotgun hammers."

The men moved up slowly, tense, some of them half drunk. Reckless. Firelight danced along gunbarrels. They stared stupidly at the tableau; the colonel caught up short by a Mexican wearing an old blanket coat.

Benreed cried, "Stand aside, boys!"

The men jerked around to stare at the big Cross Hammer foreman. Their ranks parted, giving Benreed an opening. He pointed his rifle at Arguello. "Stand away from him, Colonel! I got him dead center!"

Chase felt a drop of cold sweat at the back of his neck. The colonel was screaming, "Luke! Put down that gun!"

Arguello said, "You stand easy, Colonel. Easy. Or you die. It would give me pleasure to kill you because of what you did to my family many years ago."

But Benreed wasn't giving up. He started edging toward deeper shadows while the rest of the crowd stood uncertainly. Seeing Benreed's movement from the corner of his eye, the colonel cried, "Goddam it, Luke! This is my life you're gambling with! He's got a shotgun on me!"

Chase sat numbly, watching, unable to believe. Had it not been for Miguel Arguello's arrival he would now be sitting on the back of that gray horse under the cottonwood. Perhaps by now swinging from the limb.

Slowly Chase got to his feet. Arguello nudged the colonel with the shotgun. "Senor, at my belt there is a knife. You will use it to free Chase Iverton."

"But—" The colonel was sweating.

The shotgun was shoved hard against him. "Senor, the weapon is filled with rusty metal. It will blow you to pieces."

The men stood rigidly. Flames leaped higher as a man threw on more brush.

"Don't anybody make a wrong move," the colonel said hoarsely.

Not a man raised a hand or even twitched a finger as the colonel reached under Arguello's coat and got a knife. Chase, hope alive in him now, turned a little. He felt the ropes fall away from his wrists. Because he had been tied for so long his arms were without feeling. The knife blade sawed through the ankle ropes. The colonel was bent almost double now in his effort to free the man he had wanted to hang. Miguel still gripped the front of the colonel's shirt, the shotgun pressed solidly against the older man's side.

For the first time Chase found his voice. "Thanks, Miguel. Thanks."

"We are not free yet," the Mexican said.

"Damn right you're not!" Benreed cried.

"Luke, Luke," the colonel wheezed. "Easy. Don't give him an excuse to kill me. This is an Arguello."

The feeling had returned slowly to Chase's arms. He picked up a saddle rope from the ground, dropped the noose over the colonel's head. He drew it tight about the brown throat. The colonel lost color.

"Do you intend to hang me!" His mouth trembled.

Chase snatched the colonel's revolver from its holster. The welcome coolness of the butt was reassuring.

"You're coming with us," he said, and pointed the gun at the colonel's throat.

"I suppose you'll shoot me dead."

"You'll ride with us," Chase said, trying to keep his voice level, "so these wolves of yours won't climb our backs."

There was a stirring among the men, an exchange of glances. Noticing this the colonel again warned them not to try anything. "Easy, boys, easy. This shotgun's nothing to fool with."

It was the one weapon a group of men such as this might fear. If a rifle or revolver had been held against

the colonel there was always the possibility that some
hothead would risk his neck and chance taking a bullet.
But shot blasting from the shortened barrels of a scattergun up close could tear half a dozen men to pieces.

At a signal from Chase they started back. He tugged
on the rope that led to the colonel's neck. The three of
them moved deeper into the shadows. The men looked
on helplessly.

"Don't come after us," Chase warned them tensely.
"Tell them, Colonel. Tell them I'll kill you sure as there's
a sunrise if one man moves wrong!"

"Stay behind, boys," the colonel said loudly. "Luke,
that includes you. Stay here with the crew. And that goes
for the rest of you!"

When Benreed, standing tall by one of the fires said
nothing, the colonel added, "Luke, that's an order!"

"I hear you, Colonel," Benreed said, and spat on the
ground. He looked around. "The rest of you pay attention to what the colonel said."

It seemed a mile to the spot where the horses were
tethered. Chase found his Flatiron roan. The colonel's
chestnut was beside it. Arguello, holding his shotgun on
the colonel, was already in the saddle.

At Chase's order the colonel mounted. There was
nothing else he could do. He was unarmed. The Mexican held a scattergun on him, and could shift it to cover
the crowd by the fires if necessary. And even if the colonel considered making a break there was the noose
about his neck; the other end of the rope was held by
Chase Iverton.

Chase got gingerly into the saddle. His breath was
tight in his lungs. He saw the firelight reflected on slick
faces. Saw the watching eyes. There had been a lot of
whisky consumed this night. There was always the possibility a reckless fool or two might make a play. Sure
the scattergun would cut some of them down. And even
the colonel would die. But Chase and Arguello would
eventually be overrun.

This was what he was thinking as they slowly backed
their horses.

A man said, "I'm damn glad Iverton got away. I was
gettin' as sick in the gut as Ed Bates did."

Chase tried to identify the speaker but all he could see

was a blur of faces. He thought the voice belonged to
Dave Franklin, but he couldn't be sure.

Where deeper shadows lay along a canyon, they urged
their horses to a lope.

"You try and get away," Chase loudly warned the colonel, "and you'll have a broken neck."

After two miles they slowed. Chase listened for
sounds of pursuit. There was only the heavy breathing of
their horses, the crunch of hoofs on the dry bed of the
stream they were crossing.

"Apparently nobody coming," Chase said.

The colonel's face was pale against the darker pattern of beard. "If you intend killing me, get it over with."

Chase said nothing. He had an urge to whip the colonel as his father had done so long ago. They climbed a
slope of shale, then moved across a mesa. Lightning
played in the distance. Thunder rumbled. The smell of
rain was carried by a strong breeze.

· The three of them were riding abreast now. Chase
leaned over and touched Arguello's arm. "How's the
head, Miguel?"

"Senor Bern had a strong right arm."

"You knew it was Bern?"

"This hombre I saw from a corner of the eye. Just before he struck me down. For a long time I lay in darkness. When I came to I told your wife that I was going
after you. I was afraid it might be a trap that this *pelado*
Dublin had set for you. I trailed you to the Cross Hammer camp. Then I waited many hours for darkness to
come. And for a chance to get close to you."

Chase swallowed. "My wife cared for the wound in
your head?"

Arguello shook his head. "She did not come out of the
house. I asked her if she would be all right while I was
hunting you. She said she had a shotgun."

Chase said nothing. So Marie had ignored his request
that she bandage Arguello's wound.

The trail they were following grew rougher. Chase
wondered what Marie's reaction would be when she
learned how close he had been to dying this night. Just
thinking about his nearness to death brought cold sweat
to his back.

"It took nerve to do what you did tonight, Miguel," he said to the Mexican.

"It was dark. There was much drinking. Nobody paid any attention to me."

The colonel hipped around in his saddle. "What plans are you two hatching for me?" he demanded.

"Too bad you never bothered to learn Spanish," Chase said. "Then you'd know."

"It is a language of pigs!"

"You may one day regret you never learned to speak it."

Chapter Thirteen

THE STORM in Mexico came closer. Occasionally the three riders halted, listening. If they were being followed there was no sign of it. Maybe their luck would hold, Chase thought. Just maybe.

The strain was beginning to tell on Chase. He felt drained. And his nerves tightened even more when from a ridge he peered back into the valley they had just crossed. He saw a flicker of light that was instantly gone. Perhaps a match lighting cigar or cigarette.

Chase licked his dry lips. "If your men try and jump us, you'll be the first one dead," he told the colonel.

False dawn faintly rimmed the eastern hills. Soon Chase began to see a few head of his Flatiron cows scattered through the brush on either side of the trail. A surge of pride swept through him. He had his life again, thanks to Miguel Arguello. He and Marie would build something here despite the odds against them.

Finally in the growing light he saw his buildings ahead, the spring grass showing green here and there at the sod roofs. Hard work and sacrifice would be necessary in order to build this ranch into something fine. But what man had gained his dreams without risk and hardship?

He rose in the stirrups and shouted, "Marie!"

There was no movement. And hardly had his shout died when he saw the empty corrals. The house door stood open. Tom Bern had stolen a few head of horses. Now the rest of them were gone. Nothing moved below at Flatiron headquarters.

Arguello had also seen this and he gave Chase a stricken glance. Passing him the coil of rope Chase said, "Keep an eye on the colonel." He spurred his roan down the long slope and into the yard.

Now he saw tracks in the dust. Shod hoofs. The imprint of built-up cowman's boots. He saw the slender indentation of a woman's high heels. There were fresh droppings in the yard. Stooping, he laid the back of a hand against one mound. They were cold, stone cold. The raiders, whoever they were, had been here hours ago.

Numbly he went into the house. His shotgun and spare rifle were gone. Blankets had been pulled from the bed. The shelf that held his supply of tinned goods had been wrenched free of the wall. As if someone in their haste to unload the shelf had pulled it from the brackets. The big iron box where he kept his ammunition was empty.

Gripped with shock he moved woodenly to the bed. Some of Marie's clothing lay on the floor as if hastily discarded. Now he studied the floor, seeing scuff marks on the hard packed dirt. As if she might have dug in her heels to brace her body as someone tried to drag her. But he couldn't be sure. The sign might be old. The mark of chair legs, perhaps.

"Marie!" he cried and the bare walls threw her name back to him. In the pit of his stomach was a growing coldness.

Miguel Arguello and the colonel stood in the doorway. The colonel's face was white as he looked around the empty room. The thick brown rope was tight at his throat.

"My God," he breathed.

Arguello said, "When I was very young once *bandidos* come to our village. There was sign very much like this. They carried off my aunt. We never saw her again."

"Bandits," Chase said hoarsely, finding his voice at last. "A bunch from across the line came up here!"

The colonel shook his fist at Chase. "It's your fault. You left her here alone!"

Chase did not even look at him. In a numb voice he said, "Horse thieves. Woman thieves."

The colonel said, a trace of hope in his voice, "Maybe they only want ransom. They know I'm rich in beef."

"If you hadn't tried to hang me," Chase reminded bitterly, "I'd have been home last night."

The colonel put a hand across his trembling mouth. "We'll have to forget the past. All that matters now is Marie."

"The sign should be easy to follow, Miguel," Chase said hopefully.

"I know every family along the river," Arguello said. "They will tell me things they will not say to an Anglo. If these are *bandidos* I will learn where they have gone."

"I hope we have more luck," Chase said glumly, "than you had in finding your aunt."

"It is different when it is an Anglo woman stolen. Everywhere they ride she will be noticed."

"I'm going with you," the colonel stated flatly. "You can trust me."

"Trusting you would put a strain on a man."

"You can trust me now. My daughter's life is at stake."

"You'd risk your neck crossing the line?" Chase said, wanting to hurt this bearded fool in order to cover his own grief. "Have you forgotten Miguel's people that you drove out of Texas so long ago?"

"Nothing matters but Marie."

Thanks to the raiders they had no change of horses, no spare ammunition. Chase had loosened his roan's cinch. Now he tightened it.

"Miguel, your friends across the river can tell us where this bunch crossed if we lose the trail. And where they are heading."

"I want this damn rope off my neck," the colonel said and tentatively lifted his hands to remove it.

"Not until we're across the line. Daughter or not, I don't trust you on this side."

"But you're willing for me to go with you."

"Only for one reason. The more of us hunt her, the better chance we'll have."

Chase ordered the colonel into the saddle. He let

some slack into the rope so the colonel could mount.
Again the colonel asked that the rope be removed from
his neck.

Chase shook his head. "Not yet. We might run into
some of your friends. I want you up short if the shooting starts."

The colonel started to mount, turning a stirrup for his
foot. Chase was thinking of how risky a hunt such as
they proposed would be in Mexico during normal times.
But these were hardly normal times. The country was in
turmoil, the forces of Benito Juárez fighting to regain
the power wrested from them by the French puppet,
Emperor Maximilian.

Suddenly Chase heard his roan whinny, saw its ears
point toward the barn. As Chase reached for his gun he
saw Arguello, in the act of mounting, collapse against
his horse. This followed by the crack of a rifle. Arguello's
mount panicked, dumping the Mexican to the ground.

Movement at the corner of the barn caught Chase's
eye. Before he could fire Arguello's lunging horse
knocked him sprawling. He struck the ground with such
force that he lost his gun.

He lay stunned, unable to rise. Dimly he heard shouts
as if from a great distance. The pound of hoofs as Arguello's horse ran away.

Gradually his vision cleared. Chase saw a rifle barrel
slanted at him. And behind the rifle was Luke Benreed's
broad face. "You busted my head at Midway Store,"
Benreed said with a tight grin. "I never forgot it!"

Instinctively Chase put a hand across his face as if to
ward off the bullet that would crash into him. But the
colonel piled into Benreed, spoiling his aim. The bullet
dug a furrow in the ground a foot beyond Chase.

"Hold up there, Luke!" the colonel cried. "We need
Iverton!" Quickly he told of Marie's disappearance.

Chase got slowly to his feet, trying to get his breath.
The wind had been knocked out of him by the plunging
horse. He slanted his gaze to his revolver that lay some
distance away. Ten yards from the gun Arguello was
crumpled on the ground, an ugly stain between his
shoulder blades.

There were two Cross Hammer men with Benreed,
Tod England and Sam Whippley. They came up, hold-

ing revolvers. England was slightly built, smooth-shaven, badly bowed in the legs. Whippley was rawboned, sunburned.

The colonel had removed the rope from his neck. He was fuming. "Why'd you do it, Luke? Goddam it, I ordered you to stay back!"

"I picked two good boys an' come after you. The rest of the crew I sent home." Benreed's yellow eyes flicked to Chase. "I figured that's what you'd want me to do."

On shaky legs Chase walked over to Arguello. The man was dead. "You shot him in the back," Chase accused.

Benreed said nothing. He still gripped his rifle and looked eager to use it.

The colonel said, "Arguello is the one who could have helped us most." His shoulders straightened and he regained a semblance of his military bearing. "We'll have to make the best of the loss. No more gunplay now. Too late to worry about Arguello."

"Life's pretty damned cheap to you," Chase snapped.

"Marie's welfare is all that concerns me now." The colonel licked at his sweated mustache, studied the tight brown face of his son-in-law. "Chase, you understand the Mexicans. You speak their language. You'll have to help us."

Chase walked over to where his revolver lay in the dirt, but Benreed beat him to it. Benreed put his foot over the weapon.

"We can't trust him, Colonel," Benreed warned. "He'll try an' kill you. I don't blame him. It's what I'd do if I come as close to a rope as he did last night."

"Chase," the colonel said earnestly, "give me your word you won't turn against us. Any of us. After Marie is found we can settle any differences."

Chase hesitated. If he refused to go along with the colonel's suggestion, what could it gain? He would be unarmed. And in a land so torn by turmoil as Mexico was now it might not be easy to find a weapon. Besides, there would be five of them; not a formidable force but one able to accomplish more than a man traveling alone.

"You said yourself that Marie's welfare matters most," Chase reminded. "I'm expecting you to keep Benreed and the other two on a tight rein."

"That I promise."

Benreed looked doubtful, but removed his foot from the revolver. They split up the arms then, the colonel taking Benreed's rifle. Chase kept the colonel's revolver.

They rode south. Chase only shrugged. Within two miles the storm struck with sudden fury. Rain slashed at them. It wet them more than river spray when they swam their horses across the Rio. Some miles south was the village of Santa Margarita. Chase remembered it from boyhood when he used to go there with his father.

The tracks they were following gradually disappeared under the impact of the driving rain. Lightning struck a rock-crowned hill not half a mile away, shaking the ground. They had a time holding in their horses.

As they continued southward Chase did some heavy thinking. Now that he was away from the scene of violence at Flatiron his mind cleared. For several miles he rode in brooding silence.

The colonel was riding to his left. Benreed and the other two Cross Hammer men were in the lead. Mud had splattered against their horses. The rain was cold.

When they slowed to climb a long slant the colonel said, "Chase, you look mighty grim."

"I'm wondering about those marks on the floor. I'm thinking they were made by chair legs after all."

"What's that supposed to mean?"

Chase did not reply.

It was mid-afternoon when they came to the village, a cluster of shacks built of mud and willow poles. Their approach had been noted, for when they rode down the single dusty street there was no one about. But Chase knew that eyes watched them from shuttered windows. These people had lived too long on the border not to recognize potential trouble in the presence of Anglos. In a cantina Chase identified himself to a fat bartender. He asked if a woman with fair hair had passed this way.

"I saw such a woman."

"She was with Anglos?" Chase asked.

"Two of them." The Mexican held up two fat fingers. "I know them. They come through here many times. But no longer are they welcome." The dark face hardened. "They are in sympathy with the *imperialistas*."

"I'm in favor of the other side," Chase said.

"Viva Benito Juárez!" the fat man cried.

The colonel had been sipping brandy, his face flushed. Benreed and the others were outside with the horses.

"For God's sake, Chase," the colonel complained, "get to the point. Ask him where Marie has been taken."

Chase ignored him. "Tell me the names of these Anglos," he said to the Mexican. "Say it in English, please, so he can hear." He jerked his head at the colonel.

The Mexican said the two men were Paul Dublin and Elmo Task.

The colonel's mouth dropped open. "Paul? You lie!" He shook a fist at the Mexican.

Chase knocked the colonel's hand down, stepped in front of him. To the Mexican he said, "You are sure about Dublin?"

"I do business with him many times. But that was before he is *imperialista*."

Chase asked the man about *El Chino* and his ranch at *Tres Caballos*. The Mexican's eyes were bleak. This Chino was also *imperialista*.

"These men I seek may go to this rancho. Tell of where I can find it."

The Mexican gave sketchy directions. The rancho was many miles to the south and east in the Del Carmen mountains. There the fighting had been very heavy in the past few days.

Chase thanked the man, then turned to the colonel. "You're the man with the money. Pay for the brandy."

Numbly the colonel dug a coin from his pocket and laid it on the bar. He was staring at Chase. "You don't seem a damned bit surprised about Dublin."

"I'm not."

"You knew all along?"

"After we crossed the river I got to thinking about it."

The colonel rubbed a hand over his face. "I—I can't believe that Paul would do this to me. The Mexican must be lying. You can't trust them to tell the truth—"

Chase got him roughly by an arm and moved him outside.

Benreed and his two companions were looking apprehensively at the shuttered windows of the house. A dog

snapped at the heels of a burro loaded with firewood.
The burro was driven by an old Mexican wearing a straw
sombrero and faded serape soaked from the rain.

He saw the Anglos gathered before the cantina and
quickened his pace, shouting at the burro. When he drew
abreast of their horses, he let his eye run over the brands.
He moved on a few paces. He halted. He looked back at
the horses again, and then at the Anglos who were
watching him.

Then he quickly maneuvered the burro into a slot between mud-walled buildings.

Benreed's yellow eyes were thoughtful. "He was
mighty interested in them Cross Hammer brands."

"So I noticed," Chase said curtly.

If the colonel was aware of the old Mexican at all he
gave no sign. Dazedly he kept saying over and over, "I
can't believe it. Paul is wild, yes. But to steal a woman—"

As they pushed south Chase found his thoughts
swinging to Jessie, sister to this *El Chino*. The fighting
had been heavy in the vicinity of their rancho, the bartender said. What had happened to Jessie? Was she able
to survive, or was she dead? This latter possibility chilled
him.

By late afternoon the storm tapered off. That night
they slept in the hills, Chase with his back to a rock,
revolver by his side.

Shortly after daybreak they came suddenly to a valley
and saw below a long file of horsemen moving south in
frantic haste. Even from this distance Chase could see
the flat-topped caps, the blue gray uniforms that stamped
the cavalrymen as *imperialistas*, followers of Maximilian.
Evidently they had been in a recent battle for many of
them were bandaged.

An hour later they heard distant gunfire. It could
mean the troopers were being attacked. Chase hoped
this was the case.

They had covered several miles when they came abruptly upon a herd of cattle being driven slowly along a
wide canyon by some ten vaqueros. Two Mexicans riding drag were the first to see the Anglos. They shouted
to the others. The riders spurred together, letting the
cattle drift. They sat their saddles, eying the Anglos.

"No use to run," Chase warned his companions. "I'll go talk with them. You stay here."

He rode down, right hand lifted in the sign of peace.

As he neared the herd his quick eye roved over the brands: the Bates 66, Dave Franklin's Spur. He felt a tightening at his throat. Maybe he had blundered into something here. Mexican rustlers. They might shoot him before he could open his mouth.

The leader was slender. There was a fresh scar at his jaw, possibly the result of a saber wound.

Chase did not mention the cows. He asked the leader in careful Spanish if he had seen a woman with pale hair in the company of two Anglos.

"Si, they come this way." The leader gave a fierce smile and looked at his men. They grinned back. The leader said, "These hombres and the woman ride to meet the ones who drive these *vacas*. Many miles from here." The Mexican waved a slim hand toward the north. "But we are there waiting for them."

Anglos had driven this herd across the river, the Mexican said, intending the beef for the government forces of Maximilian. In the fierce fight that followed the Anglos had been slaughtered. All save the two with the woman, who had arrived just as the firing started.

"This man Dublin," the leader said, his eyes dangerous, "you hunt for him. He is a friend, of course." The Mexican waited. His men gripped their rifles. There was a tense silence. Down the valley the cows were searching for grass.

"He is no friend of mine," Chase said. "I seek this Dublin. I intend to kill him."

For a moment the Mexican studied the face of this Texan. Then he smiled. *"Buena suerte, good luck."*

When Chase rejoined the colonel and the others he was sweating. He told them about the cattle.

The colonel shook his head. "Rustlers must've hit the camp Bates and Franklin had—"

"Hit them while you had everybody at the Cross Hammer camp to watch your Roman spectacle," Chase said bitterly, and had a sudden urge to hit the colonel in the face. "Paul did a good job of it. He got beef, horses, and a woman."

The colonel gave him an angry glance. "Sometimes I wonder if you give much of a damn whether Marie's missing or not."

Chapter Fourteen

FOR SEVERAL MILES Chase kept watching their back trail to make sure the vaqueros didn't change their minds and ride them down. But they were apparently too pleased with their acquisition of Anglo beef to worry about them.

Tod England's horse wore out a shoe on rock after a steep climb. It began to go lame. England was worried. "This is sure no place for an Anglo to be set afoot." He turned to the colonel. "We'll get fresh hosses, won't we?"

The colonel seemed preoccupied. He was staring at the mountains ahead.

Chase said, "Cross Hammer is loved like the plague down here. Don't wonder you're worried, England. But we won't abandon you, eh, colonel?"

The colonel looked up blankly. Apparently he had been unaware of England's predicament.

They rode for many miles. Twice they had to hide in thickets when they saw large groups of riders approaching. The last outfit wore no uniforms. They were a ragtag column of some hundred men, Mexicans in wide-brimmed hats, rifles slung by shoulder straps. They dragged two cannon in their wake. Soldiers of the elected government of Benito Juárez their power usurped by the upstart Maximilian, puppet of France.

Later Chase and his party paused at the lip of a mesa. Below in the valley was a spot of green, perhaps a village or rancho.

Because England's horse was about done, they told him to follow them slowly. They would go ahead. Perhaps by the time he caught up with them they would have fresh horses. Chase tried to sound more hopeful than he felt.

They came to a village or what was left of it. There had been a garrison here. The walls were broken from cannon fire. There were fire-blackened windows. A Gatling gun, the muzzle shattered, was lying in the wreckage of a wagon.

There were no dead—probably hastily buried, Chase reasoned. But neither were there any living. The survivors of this village must have taken to the hills.

Chase looked around grimly. He advised them to get away quickly. The troops that shelled this village might return. "We don't want to be found here."

"England's out of luck," Benreed said. "No hosses here. His won't last five miles. Let's go on without him."

"He'll ride double," Chase said flatly.

Benreed and Whippley and the colonel stared at him in surprise. "These horses are about finished now!" the colonel said furiously. "They can't carry double!"

"England will change mounts every mile or so," Chase snapped. "In that way no one horse will take all the burden."

The colonel gave Chase an angry look. "Since when do you worry about a Cross Hammer man?"

"England means nothing to me personally. But he's a human being."

They started retracing their steps. There was no sign of England approaching. Chase reasoned that the man should have been halfway to the burned-out village by now.

A half hour later they found him sprawled beside his dead mount. Both man and animal had been shot, England in the mouth. And into this gaping hole had been stuffed a foot-square piece of hide cut from the dead horse. The part of the hide that bore the Cross Hammer brand.

The three riders sat their saddles without speaking. Not too long ago the dead man had been one of them. And then his horse went lame and he was left behind.

The tracks of a single rider led north.

The colonel finally recovered. "Who would do a foul trick like this?" he demanded.

"The brand cut from the horse," Chase said, feeling sick at his stomach. "It means one thing to me."

"Arguellos!" the colonel seemed shaken. He looked fearfully around at the mesa, the high rocks, the tawny land below. A hawk's wing cut blackly against a filmy cloud. Buzzards began to circle overhead. There was no time to bury England or even to pile rocks on the body to save it from animals. For many miles Chase had had the feeling that they were being followed. There was never any evidence of this, however. Just a feeling.

But now—

As they rode away he looked back, seeing man and horse crumpled, shapeless upon the ground. Tod England, drifter, had probably considered himself fortunate to sign on with an outfit the size of Cross Hammer. And because his employer, Colonel Josh Herrick, had years ago driven the rightful owners of Cross Hammer from their land, he had forfeited his life. Forfeited it by riding a horse with the wrong brand on it.

That evening they killed a cow, not risking a shot, but knifing it. They ate the stringy meat raw because to light a fire might bring them trouble. It was dangerous for troops of either side to come and look them over.

Next day the flies got into the meat they had packed with them and they were forced to throw it away.

Their luck was running out. The deeper they got into Mexico the greater the hazard of contact with the warring factions. And in addition to this hazard was the knowledge that one of their party had already died at the hand of an Arguello.

"How much longer will it take to find them?" the colonel said. He sounded unutterably weary.

"I'm betting they'll be at Chino's ranch," Chase answered. "We ought to be there by tomorrow."

"Do you think we'll ever find Marie alive?" the colonel said brokenly.

"I hope so." Chase clenched his teeth. "I want them both alive. Very much alive."

Chapter Fifteen

JESSIE THORPE watched the column of black smoke in the distance flatten out above the trees. "They've put the torch to everything!"

Her brother, Mike—*El Chino* to the Mexicans—turned in the saddle of a fine Jalisco pony. The tip of his peg leg rested in a special stirrup. "The bastards," he said under his breath. "I worked ten years to build that place."

Jessie put her dark blue gaze on her brother. "I told you a long time ago. The Mexicans don't want Maximilian."

"It isn't who wants what. I picked the side I thought would win. It seems I was wrong."

They started riding again, higher into the mountains. Around them jagged rocks rose crookedly into the sky. There was a flash of silver ahead as sunlight touched a cascading stream. There were ten other riders in the party, seven men and three women. Two of the women were Mexican. The third woman was Marie Iverton. Flanking her were Paul Dublin and Elmo Task.

Chino's hat was gone. His shaggy hair was uncombed. He needed a shave. There was a bad cut on the back of his left hand. Making sure the other members of the party were not within earshot Chino swung his horse next to the black mount Jessie was riding. "Have you still got a gun," he whispered.

"I have." She patted the pocket of her leather riding skirt.

His round face was grim. "Jessie, I want your promise. If they take us—"

"I know. Kill myself."

"If I'm alive I'll do it for you."

She gave him a long look. "Our father dead at Gettysburg. Our brother Bob killed at Cedar Mountain. Our brother Jim—the good Lord alone only knows what happened to Jim." Tears came to her eyes. "And I came down here to Mexico. To try to save my last brother. Try and make him realize that this bloody business—"

"Jessie, I didn't want you to come. Remember that."

"I didn't do much saving, did I?" She gave a hopeless laugh. "Now you talk of killing me. In the event you're still alive, of course. If you're dead I am to do the job myself."

"Don't jest," he snapped.

"I understand," she said. Her handsome face was pale. She nodded in the direction of Marie, riding ahead. "And will you give her the same advice?"

"That's up to Dublin. I don't give much of a damn what happens to her."

They came at last to a steep road that climbed to a shelving of rock halfway up a cliff. The edge of the cliff was lined with high boulders, making it a natural fortress. There were several rock shacks built around a springs. Once this had been used as an outlaw hangout. But Chino had appropriated it for his own use in case he ever had to flee *Tres Caballos*. And this he had been forced to do.

The two Mexican women started preparing a meal while some of the men cut wood. The rest of them sat around and talked, and watched the approach of darkness.

Chino had a bottle of mescal. He would drink, then look at Paul Dublin who sat across from him on the dirt veranda that fronted the largest of the structures.

At last Chino said, "You talk a big wind, Paul."

Dublin had been whispering to Marie, who sat with legs dangling over the edge of the porch. She wore a man's shirt, torn at the shoulder. Her levis, much too large at the waist, were a snug fit at the hips. Her face was sunburned. She was trying to comb the snarls out of her long yellow hair.

"I couldn't help it if everything went wrong," Dublin grunted.

"You said you knew where to lay hands on rifles and ammunition—"

"I told you. The colonel wouldn't say where they had it cached."

"You ever hear of feet in a hot fire?"

"You talk worse than a savage!" Jessie cried at her brother.

"Keep out of this, Jessie!" Chino turned his burning gaze on Dublin. "Why didn't you make him tell you where he kept the guns?"

"He's Marie's father. I couldn't go against him on that account."

"You sure spout holy talk!" Chino sneered. "Worried about her father. But you don't mind stealin' his daughter!"

"It wasn't stealin'! She come of her own free will. Didn't you, Marie?"

Marie looked around. "Yes—" Then she saw Jessie looking at her. "Well, I came because my husband was dead. What else was there for me to do?"

Jessie wore a black shirt. Her leather riding skirt was black, as were her boots. She got to her feet, white half-moons of pressure at the corners of her wide and lovely mouth. "Haven't you ever heard of burying a husband? Of mourning for him? What sort of woman are you anyway?"

The tip of Marie's pink tongue flicked along her lower lip. "I was lonely and afraid."

"I only saw Iverton once," Jessie said, her voice shriller than she intended. "But he struck me as being a man. A man for a woman to tie to. A man with more nerve than the lot of you!"

"And you helped kill him, Dublin." Jessie clenched her fists. "You harassed him in mean little ways. Sending Bern to kill a cow whenever you wanted fresh meat. Sending Bern to steal his horses so you'd have a chance to steal his wife. Oh, don't worry, I've heard you talking about it."

"That's a goddam lie!" Dublin flared.

Chino gave him a warning look. "Don't swear in front of my sister!"

Elmo Task got to his feet. He came toward the porch of the shack. He put his cold eye on Chino. "You're the one talkin' the big wind now, Chino," he said quietly. "Keep your voice down."

Chino looked at him for a long moment. Jessie felt the strong beat of her heart. When her brother was half-drunk as he was now, he could do or say anything. Consequences meant nothing. She knew Task was a gunman. Everyone at *Tres Caballos* had been afraid of him. And she knew her brother was aware of this. But her brother didn't seem to care now. He'd suffered so many disappointments. Leaving home and coming here years ago, and making a life. Because he had fought a duel over a woman and the ball from the pistol of his antagonist had struck the right knee. Gangrene had set in and the leg was amputated. In bitterness he had come to Mexico. And when the rest of her family was wiped out in the war, Jessie came to join him.

And now the fine ranch that was the pride of his life

lay in ruins. His horses and cattle driven off, his buildings burned to the ground. All that work for nothing. He had fought against the people of Mexico, because he considered this the thing to do. This would be the way to make money. He had tried to raise an army of his own to help the cause of the *imperialistas*.

These men, poorly armed, were slaughtered at *Las Casitas*. And now her brother was a fugitive. Unless the forces of Maximilian came here, which was unlikely. They were busily engaged elsewhere and could find little reason to fight in this remote area.

"You were goin' to bring guns," Chino accused Dublin. "You were goin' to bring horses. Cattle. What did you bring? You brought yourself and a runaway wife. And a gunman who's too old for usefulness—"

Elmo Task said, "You want to prove that last point?"

Jessie looked quickly in the direction of the cook fires. "I think supper's ready."

It broke the tension.

After supper Chino said that Dublin and Marie should share the main house with Jessie and him. Each of them would take a corner of the large room.

Jessie protested but her brother was adamant on this point. "Dublin's a fool over that woman, but he's a good fighter. If we have trouble I want him near me. And I want you nearby. Remember what I told you today. Don't let yourself be taken prisoner."

She went to bed, lying fully clothed in her blankets. Dublin and her brother sat up in the darkness, drinking, arguing.

At last her brother, drunk, fell asleep. He snored loudly. Jessie tried to sleep. She could hear Dublin and the woman talking in a far corner of the darkened room. The woman had a whining voice. She wondered how Iverton had been able to stand it.

"You call this luxury?" Marie was saying. "I came with you because you told me how rich we'd be. We'd own half the state of Chihuahua, you said."

"Marie. Everything went wrong."

"You said I'd ride in a fine coach and have a big house in Chihuahua City."

"Shut up!"

"Don't talk to me like that."

"Shut up!"

There was a startled exclamation from the woman. Then she began to sob. Jessie turned her face to the wall in disgust.

Marie quit sobbing and whispered, "Paul—Paul—"

"Marie."

Sounds came from them and Jessie felt her cheeks redden with embarrassment. At last came the quiet.

Animals, Jessie thought. They're nothing but animals. Her husband is dead and they are here together—

In the morning Jessie was at the springs washing her face when Marie sauntered up from the house. The sun was warm. There was a chattering of birds in the rocks above the mesa. It was hard to realize that death was so close.

Jessie got to her feet, eying Marie. She wiped her face on a bandanna. "Widowed one day," Jessie said thinly, "a bride the next."

"I am going to marry Paul. Just as soon as we can find someone to perform the ceremony. If it's any of your business, that is."

"Oh. I presumed after last night that you were already married."

Marie bared her small teeth. "You speak as if you've had experience in such things."

Jessie matched her smile. "I'm only an observer. The experience will come when and if I ever get married." She turned, her leather skirt whipping about her legs, and walked away.

Marie glared at her slender back.

Dublin came up, observing the tight anger on Marie's face. He asked her what was the matter. "I hate that bitch," Marie said.

Dublin turned to watch Jessie cross the clearing, her dark head held high. "She's a prime lookin' woman."

"I don't care for that observation," Marie snapped. "What do we do now, Paul? You talked me into coming down here with you. I have less than I had at Flatiron."

Across the clearing some of the Mexicans were cleaning their guns. Others were in the rocks at the edge of the wide shelf, watching for any approach of the enemy from the valley below. Above them a sheer cliff caught the morning sun. An eagle soared, dipped behind a jutting spire of rock where white clouds were torn by the wind.

"I been thinkin'," Dublin said. "Chase is dead. Thanks to your pa's hangrope. Maybe it's time we went home. I figure we could talk to the colonel an' he'd likely forgive us both."

She gave him a hard look. "You know how I feel about my father. I'd rather do most anything than ask him to take us in."

"If that pool herd hasn't left yet, I could go to Kansas with it. I could maybe rep for the colonel."

"And what about me?" she demanded petulantly.

"It would be a hard trip, but we'd take a wagon. We'd have ourselves a time when we got to Kansas."

"Thank you no." She ran a hand over her face that felt leathery to the touch. "I've had enough of hard trips. I need some of that luxury you promised."

"Will you stop it? How did I know things was goin' to turn out like this?"

"You were so certain of this Chino."

"We just gambled wrong. Hell, Marie, it ain't the end of the world."

"Not for you, perhaps." Her chapped lips twisted. "What about me? By now everybody in the Bend will know I ran away with you. Ran away the same night my husband died. How do you suppose they'll feel about that?"

"You didn't give much of a damn when you ran off with me," he reminded gruffly.

She stared up into the handsome face, which was a little drawn now. "You said we'd spend the rest of our lives here in Mexico, living like the *ricos*. But I've seen no rich living. Only peon living."

"Chase used to take your sharp tongue," Dublin said. "I'm not like Chase. I'll take just so much of it."

"Don't threaten me," she warned. And then she saw the hardness in his eyes. Dublin turned abruptly and started away. A quick fear touched her. Without him she would truly be alone. She ran after him.

"Paul, don't be angry. I'm just upset."

He looked down at her. "You better remember that you got nobody but me. Nobody in this whole damn world but Paul Dublin." He leaned close. "It's a far piece back to Texas. You'd have a time makin' it without me."

When Chino hobbled up on his crutch Marie went back to the spring to wash her face and hands.

Chino gave Dublin a dark look. "I heard you last night. You and the woman. Don't you have the decency to wait until you're by yourselves?"

"When a man's liable to get his brains blowed out by a Mex firin' squad," Dublin said, "he takes what's handy. As often as he likes."

"Not in front of my sister. Not tonight. Not any night. You hear?"

"What's so special about Jessie? She figure to be a nun or somethin'—"

Chino's crutch came whistling up, aimed at Dublin's head. But Dublin managed to twist aside and take the heavy blow on his shoulder. It knocked him down. Flat on his back, he reached for his gun. But Chino's revolver was already out. Chino had the crutch back under his arm. His Mexicans came running up.

Elmo Task elbowed his way through the crowd just as Dublin got to his feet. Task, his bowed legs wide, stood with his hand over his gun.

Chino gave the little gunman a hard smile. "Try it, Task," he goaded, and shifted his revolver to cover him.

The little man stared at Chino's revolver. Then he lifted his gaze to the wide face. "No man's fool enough to draw against a cocked gun," Task said.

Dublin was fingering his right shoulder where the crutch had struck him a stunning blow. "Reckon this finishes us," he told Chino.

"We should have been finished months ago. Dublin, you're a snake. Take your woman and your banty rooster gunhand and get out."

Elmo Task went white. "Don't ever come back to the States. I'll be watching for you."

Dublin gave the little man a warning shake of the head. "Don't press it, Elmo. He can have these Mexes shoot us to pieces if he's a mind."

"You must be readin' my mind," Chino said.

Jessie stepped between Dublin and her brother. "Let them go," she told him. "We've had enough bloodshed." Her pretty face was taut with strain.

Within ten minutes Dublin and Task saddled their

horses and a mount for Marie. They rode down the
steep trail from the shelving of rock.

When they were gone Chino said, "Maybe I was a fool
to let them go."

"Better than killing him."

"Let's hope Dublin doesn't meet up with some *juaristas*. They'd like to know about this hideout."

Jessie stared at the faint cloud of dust left by the departing trio. "This should convince you," she told her
brother, "that there is nothing left for us in Mexico. Let's
go back to the States."

"The war isn't done yet," Chino said. "We can still
win." He gave Jessie a faint smile. "I'll get you to the
border. That's one thing I will do."

"We still have the mine our father left us."

Chino sneered, "The Great Eagle Mine. There isn't
enough silver there to keep me in whisky."

"But it would be something," Jessie said, looking
around. "Better than this. Anything is better than this."

Chapter Sixteen

IN THE COLD light of an early day Chase Iverton stared
at the ruins of *Tres Caballos*, the gutted buildings, the
dead livestock. The gluttonous *zopilotes*, the buzzards,
heavy from their scavenging could hardly fly. They beat
their black wings and made strange sounds of protest
at this interruption.

On the ground lay a woman's dress, half burned from
the fire. A stab of fear went through Chase when he
thought of Jessie and what this carnage might have
meant to her.

The colonel looked sick. Not because of the ruins, but
because they had not found Marie.

They were in the high mountains and it had rained
recently. There were no fresh tracks. Scouting the area
Chase found a trail that led eastward. It was as good a
one as any to follow, he thought. If there had been any
survivors at all they would probably follow a trail such

as this that appeared to lead to higher elevations where the country would be rough and fugitives harder to find.

Again, as they moved along this trail, Chase had the feeling that they were being followed. But he saw no one when from a promontory he looked back the way they had come.

Benreed and Whippley were all for turning back immediately. The sooner they reached Texas again, the better they would feel.

"Go ahead," Chase told them gruffly. "I'll push on alone."

"Chase, I'm with you," the colonel said, and glared at his men. "They'll come along with us!"

Within half an hour they climbed a quarter of a mile. Above them the cliffs crowded in so that their view of the sky was reduced to a slit between overhanging walls of rock.

Because of the narrow trail they traveled single file. To their right rose a mountain, its slopes covered with pines. On the left there was a sheer drop of some thousand feet. Chase leaned in the saddle and peered below. A creek, looking like a silver wire because of the distance, flowed through a canyon. There was a gone feeling in the pit of his stomach. One misstep on the part of his horse and a man would go plunging into oblivion. This was the sort of trail where a man would be safer on a mule.

A deer bounded suddenly from a thicket above the trail. It went scampering up the steep slope to a higher elevation. The abrupt appearance of the animal sent a quiver through the horses. The four riders halted, ready to swing down if any of the animals started to buck. But after a moment they quieted.

The colonel was in the lead. He looked back, his face gray above his beard. "That sort of thing gives a man the shakes," he said, and peered over the edge of the cliff.

Chase was bringing up the rear. "No harm done this time," he called. "Let's hope nothing else spooks them."

Benreed, riding directly in front of Chase, said nothing. Whippley was next in line. He rode with toes barely in the stirrups, ready to jerk out his feet and quit the saddle if trouble developed.

They moved slowly, climbing. The air was thin. Sunlight spearing through clouds had little warmth. This seemed to be a primitive country. No sign of a rancho, or even an Indian village. Nothing. Just the deer they had seen earlier.

They had gone no more than a mile when a rider appeared suddenly on the narrow trail ahead. A Mexican, judging from his wide-brimmed hat, the faded serape across his shoulders. He rode with head down, apparently paying no attention to the trail. He gave the appearance of dozing in the saddle of his mule.

Because of the narrowness of the trail here it was impossible to pass. Somebody would have to give way. The colonel gestured angrily at the Mexican, who had reined in the mule some fifty feet up the trail and was watching them.

"Hey," the colonel shouted, "back up that mule!"

The rider came on slowly again, drawing nearer to the lead horse ridden by the colonel.

The colonel twisted around in the saddle. "Chase, you speak their language! Tell this Mex he's got to back up till we find a turnout."

They had halted their horses now. The Mexican was within ten feet of the colonel. Chase, standing up in the stirrups said loudly, "Senor, will you do us the favor—"

That was as far as he got. The Mexican had slipped from the back of his mule. In the same movement he drew the serape from his shoulders. He stepped in front of his mule and whipped an end of the serape across the eyes of the major's horse.

With a springing leap the colonel's mount cleared the trail. It sailed, squealing, out into space. One chill scream burst from the colonel's lips. As he began to fall he jerked free his feet from the stirrups. As if that would help him now. Horse and rider dropped swiftly. The colonel fought the rush of air around him with hands and feet. Within the space of twenty heartbeats the colonel and his horse were gone.

Chase was out of the saddle, holding his roan. It was skittish, trying to rear. The screams, the frightened sounds made by the horse sent a tremor through the other mounts. Benreed and Whippley had dismounted, holding their horses up close. Benreed had lost his hat.

Up the trail the Mexican stood in front of his placid mule. He still held the serape. Now that Chase got a better look at him he could see that he was an old man.

With one hand Benreed quieted his horse, drew his revolver with the other. "Whippley, duck down," Benreed said through his teeth, "an' give me a shot at that loco bastard."

Chase pointed his revolver at Benreed's back. "Don't touch him!" Chase warned. "I mean it!"

Benreed looked around. His mouth tightened when he saw the weapon leveled at his back. "This Mex killed the colonel. He damn near finished us along with him. Now you want to save his hide."

"Benreed, put up the gun. A gunshot might spook these horses for sure."

Whippley licked his lips. "He's right, Luke."

With an oath Benreed holstered his weapon.

The Mexican had mounted his mule. "I beg forgiveness," he said in Spanish, "if I risk frightening your horses also, but—" He spread his dark hands. "I am a man possessed. Such a man does not consider the risk to others."

Chase studied the wrinkled brown face. "I remember you. You had a burro loaded with firewood at the village of Santa Margarita. You looked long and carefully at the horses branded Cross Hammer. You've been trailing us."

"I know these mountains. I come ahead by another trail and wait for you."

"And you killed one of our companions. Shot him and stuffed horsehide into his mouth."

"This I do not do. But I hear of it from a relative who is older than I am."

"Your name is Arguello."

"That is the name," the old man said. "I have waited years for revenge."

"Do you think Colonel Herrick recognized you?"

The Mexican's shoulders shrugged under the serape. "A man changes with age. I was younger, much younger when he drove me off my rancho and killed many members of my family."

"Get out, old man," Chase said, and gestured up the trail with his revolver. He was sweating.

Without a word the Mexican backed his mule along the narrow trail. At a place a hundred yards up trail there was a place where he could turn his mount. In a moment he was gone, out of sight around a jutting shoulder of rock.

Benreed expelled a long-held breath. "I don't savvy this, Iverton. You let him get away with killin' the colonel. So he's an Arguello. What of it?"

"Poetic justice, I guess. An old wrong righted. And without even firing a gun. Much more personal revenge."

"You don't give much of a damn that the colonel's dead."

"Not much."

Whippley was looking over the edge of the cliff. Far below on the rocks were two faint brownish spots.

"Get uptrail," Chase ordered the two men. Benreed and Whippley mounted and rode to where the Mexican had turned his mule. Here was a small clearing against a cliff. There was a blackened fire ring and dead ashes.

Chase did not ride to the clearing. He walked, leading his horse. He still gripped his gun. If Benreed or Whippley tried anything he wanted both feet on solid ground for accurate shooting.

"What now?" Benreed said.

"You and Whippley get out." Chase gestured in the direction they had taken from *Tres Caballos.* "I'm going on alone."

"We been with you this far," Benreed said.

"I trusted you little enough with the colonel alive. I trust you even less with him dead."

"I see." Benreed gave a small hard smile.

"You might as well know this. When I've settled with Paul Dublin I'll be looking for you. I haven't forgotten that you killed Miguel Arguello. Shot him in the back."

Benreed slanted his yellow eyes at Whippley, who slouched in the saddle, tired, surly. "You can settle it now, Iverton," Benreed said, "if you're a mind. Put up the gun. We'll go at it even."

Chase shook his head. "I'm not fighting the two of you. I don't want to chance dying until I settle with other people."

"Your wife and Dublin." Benreed's lips curled. "I went through the war with Dublin. We fought under the colonel. I know Dublin. He's a hellion with the ladies. Know what I think? I think your wife run away with Dublin. I don't think she was kidnapped at all—"

Chase centered his gun on Benreed's broad chest. "You mean less to me than dirt. Open your mouth about my wife again and I'll kill you."

There was no venom in the voice, no hysteria. It was just a simple statement made by a man who meant what he said. Benreed licked his lips. He jerked his head at Whippley. The two of them rode back down the steep trail, Benreed in the lead.

Chase stood a moment, feeling spent. What did the colonel's death mean to him? He tried to dredge up some feeling for the man, but found it hard to do. What would Marie say when he finally found her—and he would find her if it took ten years. Would she show any grief over her father's tragic passing? Or was she incapable of any emotion whatsoever?

He looked back down the trail, seeing its narrowness, the sheer drop on one side, the cliffs on the other; a crooked shelving that disappeared in the distant rocks.

Benreed had wanted to return to Texas. This was his chance. He wondered if the two men would ever make it back to the border. They knew only a few words of Spanish. A man needed to understand the Mexicans, to speak their language in times like these. Even then you could find the end of your life awaiting you in a shallow Mexican grave.

He pushed on, seeing a branch trail that led up from the western slopes, and knew this was likely the one taken by the old Mexican when the man realized they were going into the mountains. The trail Chase followed climbed higher. There was no sign of life. The desolation depressed him.

A single distant rifle shot alerted him. He drew his revolver and waited. The shot was not repeated. He stared down at the gun in his hand. It had belonged to the colonel and had been taken from him the night at the Cross Hammer camp when a hanging had been interrupted. How much death since that night? Miguel Arguello, Tod England, and now the colonel. All because he, Chase Iverton, had come back to Texas.

He let down the hammer and returned the weapon to

his holster. Tiredly he ran a hand over his jaws, feeling a bristle of beard. Had anything at all been accomplished by this mad dash into Mexico? By pressing ahead would he find Marie? Or would the trail become a dead end?

As he started moving uptrail again the wind increased. It whistled along the draws and through stunted pines. The trail left rock and angled across a park.

Suddenly he came through a stand of junipers. Not twenty yards ahead in a clearing was Paul Dublin. Dublin held a knife. He was bent over a buck deer, using the knife to cut away the hind quarters. Spread out on the grass was a tarp that undoubtedly would serve as a wrapping for the meat. Dublin looked harassed, and his face was thinner than Chase remembered.

All this seen in the space of seconds. The sudden appearance of Chase Iverton seemed to freeze Dublin. He remained hunched over the deer, his mouth open. Sunlight lancing through the junipers touched the blade of the knife. On the ground beside Dublin was a rifle.

In that moment Chase recalled the rifle shot he had heard earlier.

Chase reached for his gun, and knew he had Dublin covered. "Where's my wife?"

There was a movement in the trees to his left. From a corner of his eye Chase saw a small man wearing a dirty shirt appear suddenly. It was Elmo Task. Before Chase could ram in the spurs, Task fired a revolver. Chase fell backward out of the saddle, firing his gun at the sky. His horse, stirrups flapping, ran off into the junipers.

There was no pain, just a numbness. He lay on his back, staring up at the sky. A quiet darkness enveloped him completely.

Chapter Seventeen

ELMO TASK TRAMPED out of the woods, holstering his revolver. "There's been too many gunshots," the little man said, looking around at the high peaks. "We better get the hell out of here. Some *juaristas* could be around here."

Dublin wiped the blade of his knife on the grass. He wrapped in the tarp the venison he had already cut from the deer. They hurried to their horses tied off in the trees. With the tarp lashed to Dublin's saddle horn they rode into the higher mountains.

At last Dublin recovered from his shock. "I told you not to leave Marie alone!"

"I seen him comin' uptrail," the little gunman said. "I figured I better sneak down and have a look. Good thing I did. He'd have cooled you sure. He had you dead center."

"I'd have got him."

"Well, he's out of the way now for sure."

"What if he isn't really dead?" Dublin grumbled. "We should've looked him over better."

"Even if he isn't dead—which is damn unlikely, he won't last twenty minutes with that hole in his chest."

Dublin was scowling. "What I can't figure is how he got away from the colonel. He was supposed to hang."

"Iverton's a lucky man."

"Not now he isn't lucky," Dublin said.

They came to a high point where Marie had been left. From here one could plainly see the trail below.

Marie looked frightened. "I heard shooting."

Dublin swung down, gave her a grim look. "You might as well know the truth. Chase didn't hang."

Her hands flew to her mouth. "You've seen him?"

"Elmo shot him. He's layin' a half mile down trail. You want to go and look at him?"

She swallowed and ran a tongue around the pale rim of her mouth. She put out a hand to a juniper trunk to steady her knees. "I want to get out of Mexico." Her face was gray. "That's all I want."

Elmo Task gave her a thin glance. "You don't seem to care much whether your husband is dead or not."

"So far as I'm concerned," she said in a shaky voice, "he's been dead for a long time. I'm sorry it had to happen this way, but—"

"You hold it against me for killin' him?" Task said.

She pushed at her pale hair. It was badly tangled. She began to sob. "I want to go home."

"Home," Paul Dublin muttered, and looked at Task. "We'll go back to Texas. We'll have a long talk with the colonel. I'll tell him Marie and me is sorry about runnin' off together."

"For all you know he may have a hundred Texans huntin' for us," Task reminded soberly. "Stealin' a woman ain't like stealin' beef, you know. An' he'll figure Marie was stolen all right."

Dublin rubbed his jaw. "Between her and me we'll get the colonel to do anything we want. How about it, Marie?"

Her shoulders sagged. "I don't want to go back to Cross Hammer, but—" She gave Dublin an angry look. "All your plans have failed. I guess there's nothing else for me to do."

At mention of his plans Dublin's face reddened. "It wasn't my fault how things turned out. Chino's the one to blame. I figured he'd have Chihuahua in his hind pocket by the time we got here."

They mounted up and Elmo Task gave Marie a strange look. "I figure it would be decent to go and bury Iverton."

"If you think that is necessary," she said, not looking at him, "you'll do it. I—I don't want to see him."

"How about it, Paul?" Task said.

"Elmo, you're gettin' soft in the gut," Dublin snapped irritably. "You're the one killed him. Not us."

"I saved your bacon by doin' it. He don't mean a damn to me. But you growed up with him." His gaze swung to Marie's drawn face. "And you was married to him. There's such a thing as decency, so they tell me."

Dublin said, "All right. We'll bury him."

They started down the slope but before they could reach the spot where Chase Iverton lay in the cool green grass, they saw horses. Riders were dismounted, peering at the man on the ground. There were six of them. One of them had only one leg. *El Chino.*

"Chase'll get his buryin' now," Dublin said. "Let's keep outa their way. I had enough of Chino to last me a lifetime."

"I've had enough of his sister," Marie said through her teeth.

Task looked back at the group in the trees far below. "They must be pullin' out."

"I don't care what they do," Dublin said. "Let's hope our luck holds till we get to the border."

They started down one of the side trails. Marie's mind was numb. Chase was dead, finally dead. He had escaped the noose prepared for him by her father. How did she feel now? This little man with the hard face who rode on her left had killed Chase. Chase Iverton, husband to Marie Herrick. Had he ever really been her husband? In the space of days she found it hard to recall what he had even looked like. It was too bad that he had the misfortune to be first home from the war. She supposed he had often thought of this himself.

It was some hours later that they ran into Benreed and Whippley. The pair had lost their way. As they rode north together Dublin told what had taken place. Then Benreed disclosed how the colonel had died.

Dublin smiled and looked around at Marie. "Looks like you own Cross Hammer lock, stock an' barrel."

Marie just stared numbly at Benreed.

"By God," Dublin said, his eyes shining, "our luck did hold at that. Marie, you'll be a rich woman."

"Yes." She pushed at her hair. "I suppose I will."

Chapter Eighteen

THE FIRST THING Chase heard was a woman's voice saying, "I thought sure he was dead."

"He's bad shot, Jessie," a man said gruffly.

"We can't go off and leave him!" Jessie cried.

"Ride him as far as we're going and it'll kill him sure."

"Then we'll take him back to the hideout."

"Are you loco, Jessie?" Chino demanded. "We can't go back there. It's a wonder the *juaristas* didn't find that place before this."

"All right, then," Jessie said, folding her arms. "You go ahead. I'll stay with him."

"What's this man to you?" her brother demanded. "You only saw him once before that I know of."

"Haven't you any decency left? Can you go off and leave a human being to die alone?"

Chino grumbled, then said, "We'll go back. But he won't last, I can tell you that. I suppose one more day won't make much difference to us one way or the other."

There was not much else Chase remembered but pain and darkness. The pain cutting like a knife. And occasionally through the blackness he saw Jessie's face. Saw the face worried by day, worried in the glow of lamplight. He felt her cool hands on him. When she bent over he caught the scent of her hair. It was dark like a cloud filled with storm.

"Hang on. Don't die on me, Iverton. I've seen too much of dying. Let this be a living, dear God. Not death."

He saw her heating a knife blade to sterilize it. Then the knife was in him and he felt the searing heat of it. He tried to hit her but his arms were weighted stones. There was the sickening odor of burned flesh. The one final shuddering gasp of pain that caught him up in terror.

He heard someone weeping and the sound was strange. Until he realized he was the one weeping. It made him think of the first time he had seen violent death. He was a boy. And there was a Mexican lying on the ground near the fire-blackened ruins of a house. His face had been shot away. Chase remembered his father's terrible voice: "Herrick did this. Why? Why does a man have to kill? Why does a man covet the land of another? Look at this man on the ground, son, and remember that greed easily turns to murder. His name was Pablo Arguello. He was an old man and he ranched here ever since there was a man on horseback in this country. Maybe descendant of one of Coronado's men who tired of pillage and came here to live a new life. And now this man Herrick kills him. All for a ranch he calls Cross Hammer."

"Shhhhh," Jessie said. "Don't talk. Sleep."

Chino said. "I got hold of a mule. We'll tie him on."

"But he's so ill."

"It's been a week. We've got to clear out."

They tied Chase to the mule and started down the

steep trail out of the mountains. Chino had only three men left. The rest had deserted. During most of the descent from the mountains Chase was irrational. The jolting ride had opened his wound. Jessie halted many times and put on a fresh bandage.

When they reached the flats the other three men deserted.

One night Chino knelt down on his good knee at the spot where Chase lay wrapped in blankets. "I've got a feeling, Iverton. Maybe the good Lord let you live so you could look after Jessie. I got the feeling I won't make it."

Chase watched the shadowed face of the one-legged man who had tried to play politics in this turbulent country.

Chino went on, "She's risked her neck for you. If anything happens to me see that she gets to the border."

"I—promise." It was difficult to speak. There seemed to be an unnatural thickness to his tongue.

They moved slowly, feeling their way. At last they saw a village ahead. Many of the roofs were burned off, walls shattered from cannon fire. The place seemed deserted.

There was a sudden shout: "Viva! Viva!" A gunshot cut through the silence. Jessie screamed. Chase, roused from dozing in the saddle of his mule, jerked his eyes open. But the mule was shying from an object in the road, a dead peon. The mule carried him under the low branch of a willow. As his forehead came in contact with the hard wood there was the sound of thunder in his brain.

He finally awakened. Voices speaking Spanish came to him. He opened his eyes and found he could move his hands. By turning his head he could look out a broken window and see some twenty men gathered around a bonfire in the street. He saw crossed bandoleers over broad chests and narrow chests. He saw rifles slung from shoulders. Sombreros of velvet, some of straw.

Beyond the campfire ringed by men he saw a fire-blackened 'dobe wall and a dead horse in the street.

He sat up, seeing that he had been lying on a long table. He looked around at broken chairs, a smashed sideboard. Once this had evidently been the parlor of a *casa*.

There had been much fighting here, one could tell. Bullets had made a lethal pattern against one 'dobe wall. There was a smear of blood on the floor. His head was pounding. He lifted a hand to his forehead. It was bandaged.

Jessie's voice reached him. "You have a hard head. You broke the willow limb."

He looked around. She sat stiffly in a chair. Her long dark hair was loose about her shoulders. She seemed despondent.

"Who are the men out there?"

"*Juaristas*. They're going to shoot you and my brother —" Her mouth trembled. Her eyes were dark and frightened. He saw the jerky movement of her breasts under the black shirt.

"They're going to turn you loose?" he said.

She just looked at him and he said, "They won't hurt you. Those are soldiers, not ruffians."

"They're *bandidos*. There is only one soldier, a Captain Morellos. He said in this war you accept help wherever you can."

There was a sudden shout from outside, much laughter. Somebody threw a bottle that shattered against the wall. Chase licked at his lips that had been seared by fever.

"Your brother. Have they—shot him?"

"He's with them. Outside." She put the tips of her fingers into her mouth and bit them.

Swinging his legs off the table he stood up. It seemed as if there was no bone in his legs, only marrow. He took a step and did not fall. He moved at a shuffling gait toward the door. As he had expected there was a *soldado* on guard there. When he saw Chase he lifted his rifle and gestured for him to go back inside.

Chase stepped back but he could see out into the street from where he stood. Glow from the campfire lighted the street. He saw a group of *soldados* coming toward the house, led by a tall Mexican wearing a velvet hat with a bullet hole in the crown. His slender, aristocratic face was taut from weariness. The *soldados* moved slowly, keeping step with the one-legged man in their midst.

In front of the house the Mexican in the velvet hat gave

his men an order, "Alto!" They halted. He and Chino entered the house.

They came to a halt when they saw Chase standing in a sort of vestibule. Chino's mouth thinned. "My luck turned sour from the day I ran into you along the river. I had a chance to shoot you. I should have taken it."

"A little late for regrets," Chase said, fighting the trembling in his voice and legs.

Chino said, "This is Captain Morellos. He—he's going to let me say good-by to Jessie."

Chase looked at the Mexican. The eyes were black, hard. "We are Yanquis," Chase said. "You have no right—"

"*El Chino* is ten years in my country," Morellos said. "There is a bounty on his head."

"This day will make you rich, eh?" Chino said, and leaned against his crutch.

"I will give the bounty to my men," Morellos said stiffly. "I do not deal in blood money." He jerked his head at the door leading to the parlor. "We will go in."

They went into the room where Jessie sat woodenly in the chair. Her face was almost drained of color. She got slowly to her feet.

"I've talked to Morellos," Chino said. "I've taken all the blame. You and Iverton did no fighting against the *juaristas*. I've convinced him of that." His gaze slid to the dark face. "Right, Morellos?"

Morellos stood with arms folded. His jacket was stained, torn under one arm. His pants and boots were muddied. He said nothing. He was looking at Jessie across the room. Chase, noticing the look, felt his stomach turn over. He lowered his gaze to the ivory-butted gun Morellos wore at his belt. If he could get his hands on that gun. He took a step forward and had to halt, to correct his balance. His legs were so terribly weak. And at a time when he needed strength more than at any period in his life.

Chino said, "Morellos is going to make it easy on you two." Chino looked at his sister. The only light in the room was from the bonfire in the street outside. "Good-by, Jessie."

There was a stricken look on her face. She started toward him, hands lifted. But Chino shook his head. "Stay where you are. No tears. I asked for this, you know."

She halted, standing rigid.

Chino turned to Chase and his eyes seemed to be trying to convey some message. But what?

"Funny," Chino said, "but you miss the little things most." He sniffed the air. "I'm going to miss the smell of the river." He gave Chase a significant look then turned and shuffled out of the room.

Morellos did not follow him. He was looking at Jessie again. In this moment she seemed to recover from her shock. She tried to run after her brother but Morellos blocked the door with his body. He told her to go back and sit down.

"Do that, Jessie," Chase said. He could feel the mighty triphammer of his heart. He wanted Jessie away from him. She gave him a blank look then turned and went numbly back to her chair and sat down.

Chase moved closer to Morellos. There seemed to be turmoil mirrored in the Mexican's eyes. Firelight spilling through the shattered window touched the ivory butt of the belt gun.

Chase kept his eyes on Morellos' face. "My father was a friend to the Mexicans. Perhaps you remember him. Ralph Iverton."

"The name means nothing to me."

Chase took another step. God he was tired. He wanted to lie down on the floor and close his eyes. "Morellos, I know what you're thinking," he said in a low, tense voice. "You've seen much bloodshed. You're bitter against men like *El Chino*. Don't take it out on his sister."

Morellos gave him a long look. "For a moment I thought you were begging for your own life."

"Don't let this thing happen to her."

"She'll face no firing squad. I'm not such a fool as to kill something as valuable as a woman."

Chase clenched his teeth. Another step. Still the gun was out of his reach. So far. And his hand as he stretched it out in an attitude of entreaty seemed heavy as iron.

Another step. *"Por favor, El Capitan—"*

"No favors," Morellos said brusquely. Whatever inner struggle had been gripping the man seemed to have been resolved. He cocked his head as a burst of shouting came from his men. "They are impatient." He said bitterly,

"I am a man of education, but those out there—" He waved a hand toward the street. "They are little more than brigands. A pretty woman, especially an Anglo woman— Well, there would be no discipline." The dark eyes bit at his face. "You understand, Senor?"

Chase felt that his face was a mask of hardened clay and if he altered his expression in the slightest degree it would shatter and fall upon the floor at his feet.

"War is never pleasant," Morellos said. "You know that from the war in your own country. There are worse things than death—for a woman."

He stepped suddenly away from Chase and moved to the table where he placed a short-barreled pistol. Beside this he laid a single cartridge. Then he came back to the door. Jessie was paying no attention. Her head was bowed.

"I do this," Morellos said still in that quiet voice, "maybe for the sake of this father you say was a friend of my people. Perhaps I do it for her brother who asked that this be so." He gestured toward the revolver on the table. "You could take that weapon with the single bullet and try to get out when I leave this room. But think carefully. My guards would kill you. And the woman would still be alive."

"I understand." Chase started moving toward him again. Toward the ivory-butted gun that would contain at least five shots.

Morellos said softly, "The one bullet. For her."

His mouth twitched. He stepped around Chase, out of reach as if sensing what was in the Texan's mind. At the door he said significantly, "I have no choice but to return for you in ten minutes. I hope by then you have taken care of certain matters."

He went out quickly, saying something to the guard at the front door. Without doubt the rear door was also guarded. A great shout went up from the men outside as Morellos strode down the street toward the campfire. Through the window he saw Chino leaning against the fire-blackened 'dobe wall across the street, crutch under his arm.

No help from him now. Nothing mattered but Jessie.

He turned toward the table. Jessie watched him, her eyes filled with terror. He walked as if in a dream.

Ten minutes, Morellos had said. Then your shoulder blades against sun-dried bricks. The rifles leveled at your breast. The quick and slashing death—

Something Chino had said spun through his mind: "I'm going to miss the smell of the river."

Chapter Nineteen

THE RIVER! That could mean one thing, the Rio. Across the river was the U. S. Texas. A long way from the Bend here, but still Texas.

He moved quickly to the table, nearly lost his balance, righted himself. His heart was pounding. He was drenched with sweat. From the street outside came another burst of shouting: "Viva Juárez!"

"Jessie, listen to me," he said hoarsely. "When we were captured. Did you notice the river?"

"I—I—" She was staring at the gun on the table and the single cartridge. As he picked up the weapon and loaded it with the single bullet, she turned away. Her hands were clenched in her lap, the knuckles white. Her whole body was stiffened as if to resist an impact. She knew what the gun meant, what the single cartridge meant. Of course she knew.

"I've got a hunch the river isn't far," he said.

He got her by an arm and with all his strength pulled her out of the chair. He began pushing her toward the back door. She resisted him, as a drowning person will struggle against a rescuer.

"Jessie, Jessie," he whispered. "Please—"

Just before he reached the door he went ahead of her and peered out cautiously. He saw a rear yard littered with trash. Flickering light from the huge bonfire in the street barely touched a 'dobe wall along one side of the yard, and a gate. The gate was open.

He glanced hurriedly at the heavens, saw the north star.

A shadow moved just beyond the door. A blocky shadow. Chase smelled smoke from a cigarillo. For a moment he could hardly make the man out, then his eyes became accustomed to the deeper shadows here. The guard had a wide-brimmed hat and a rifle slung from a shoulder strap. His back was to the door. He was looking toward the street, standing on tiptoe so he could see over the wall that surrounded the yard.

There was a sudden rattle of rifle fire from the street. The guard said under his breath, happily, "*El Chino!*" He laughed. The laughter broke off and he turned quickly as Chase came out the doorway. Before the man could lift his rifle Chase struck savagely at the face with the whole frame of the gun Morellos had left for him.

He felt a nose give way, heard a sob of pain. Then the man dropped. He looked for more guards. The man seemed to have been alone. There was the one at the front of the house but the firing, the shouting from the street drowned out their escape through the back door.

Snatching up the rifle of the unconscious *soldado* Chase got Jessie by the arm again, forced her at a crazy run across a yard. Her mind seemed numb from shock. Twice she tried to get away from him and turn back.

Each time he caught her, tearing the sleeve of her shirt the last time. "My brother," she would say in a dazed voice. "My brother."

"He's beyond help now! Run, Jessie. Run!"

He propelled her northward. Behind them was shouting, laughter. Somebody banged a guitar and there was singing.

Yes, there was the clean sweet smell of the river in his nostrils. His heart leaped. Ahead loomed willows. He tripped over a root and fell. He picked himself up, shakily. He got Jessie moving again. Her hair was wild about her face.

"Can you swim!" he cried.

She did not answer.

Far behind them was a shout, this one of anger, not pleasure. There was a gunshot. He heard somebody cry, "Yanqui!" and knew it applied to them.

They staggered through deep sand. His lungs burned. There was a pulsating red light across his vision. Then he felt water about his legs. He staggered out into the river, pushing Jessie. He felt the current suck at his weakened legs. He saw Jessie's dark head go under.

Desperately he lunged for her. He got a handful of dark hair, pulled her to the surface.

Behind them was a pounding of hoofs. He looked back, but because of the darkness and the willows could see nothing. More shouting. A rifle slug went whistling across the river, far wide of its mark. They were shooting blindly.

Suddenly the last of his strength was gone. He felt himself sinking. His own plight seemed to shake Jessie free of the icy terror that had gripped her. He saw the pale oval of her face close to his. Felt her hands on him.

"Fight, Chase!" she cried. "Fight!"

He struggled desperately while she tugged at him. He had long ago lost the rifle. He beat the water with his hands and feet. At last he felt sand under his feet. She literally pulled him the last dozen yards. They both sank exhausted upon the sand. Across the river the shouting moved eastward. There was more firing. Farther away now.

"We've got to get away," he panted.

They got up and with arms about each other for support struggled through dense thickets. They climbed a low hill. At last they found a shelter of sorts in some rocks. Here they warmed each other by pressing close, for their clothing was soaked and the night was not warm.

In the first light he opened his eyes. He removed his arm from under her shoulders. She looked up at him, a faint smile on her lips. Then she picked up the revolver he had slept beside all night. She broke the weapon open and ejected the single shell. She held the bullet in the palm of her hand.

"I thought you were going to shoot me," she said. "I don't know which terrified me the most. Dying or being left alive."

"We got away. It's your brother we have to thank."

"Poor Mike." She closed her eyes. "Those rifle shots just as we left the house—" She looked at him.

Chase nodded. "I expect they were for him."

He put his arm out and she came to him and cried softly against his chest.

At last she drew back. "Promise me, Chase. Promise

me that you'll never take a gun to another human being as long as you live."

He got to his feet and pulled her up. "We better be moving. We need food."

She looked at him for a long moment, brushing damp hair out of her eyes. "Didn't you hear what I said?"

He was looking around at the hills, the river flowing behind them. The sheet of water glistened in the new day. Far across the river he could see a wisp of smoke through the willows. Perhaps the smouldering ruin of a building. Or a cook fire. He wondered if they would risk crossing the river to search for them now that they could follow tracks by daylight. It was possible, but not likely.

"This country looks familiar," he said. His head ached intolerably. "I think we're a little east of Rivertown. I came through here once when I visited Paso."

They started walking. They spoke little. Their clothing dried at last. His legs felt heavy, heavier. He felt as if he could not move another step, yet he kept on. The day was going to be a scorcher, he thought. And this so early in the spring. Then he felt the feverish taste in his mouth. Jessie was looking at him oddly.

They had been climbing a long slant. Now below he saw some buildings.

"Rivertown," he said, and his voice was strangely distant.

For a time he remembered nothing. Then he saw the sun in his eyes and knew he lay on his back. Jessie was weeping. "You exhausted yourself."

Then there was the sound of a wagon, and then a jolting ride. Later a fat man with a watch was holding his wrist. He felt cool sheets and wondered at this luxury. He was in a small room with unpainted walls. He saw a cracked water pitcher on a shelf and a basin with a swan on it. And there was a small stove.

"It's pneumonia, ma'am," the fat man said, "near as I can tell. I doctored more hosses than humans, but reckon I'm not too far wrong on this. Both lungs are filled with fluid." He gave a shake of his head. "I don't like it."

When the fat man had gone Jessie came to the bed and looked down. "I've sent a letter to Red. He'll be down from the mine and drive us up. The mountain air will be wonderful for you, Chase."

Each day Jessie was gone for several hours. She would come home carrying an apron, a package of food under her arm. One day when Chase could sit up she said she no longer had to work at the Emporium Cafe, waiting table. She said Red had arrived and brought back some money.

"I'll pay you back, Jessie," Chase said. "You've been good to me. Better than anyone ever was in my whole life."

"We'll leave for the mine in the morning. You're so much better now, I don't·think the trip will tire you—"

"I think I'll stay here, Jessie," Chase said. "You'd better go on alone."

For a moment her face changed. There was a knock at the door. A heavy-set man in his fifties entered. He had a red beard and a spring steel handclasp. He was Red Ingalls who ran a small silver mine in the Mogollons of New Mexico. Now that Jessie was the only member of her family left alive, she was sole owner.

"Red, thanks for coming," Jessie said soberly. "I'll stay here with Chase."

Red Ingalls gave them both a careful scrutiny. "Old Pedro can run the Great Eagle mine for a spell." He forced a laugh. "Ain't much great about it no more, Iverton. Seems like the Spaniards got most of the silver. But—" He turned to Jessie. "I'll stay a spell myself."

Jessie bit her lip. "This house is so small—"

"You fix our meals. Me an' Iverton will bunk at the hotel. How about it?" He clapped Chase on the back with false heartiness.

"Suits me," Chase said carefully. "I won't be here long anyway. I'll be getting back to the Bend."

Before Jessie could say anything, Red put in, "You better set in the sun for a spell, young fella. The doc says there's no good reason why you should be alive. But a lot of good reasons why you should be dead. Jessie's cookin' will put some tallow on you."

Jessie seemed reluctant to see them go to the hotel. But Red explained that it would look better. They rode to the hotel in the wagon. They got their room and Red gave Chase the bed and had a cot moved in for himself.

"I'll repay you," Chase said. "I have cattle. I'll sell them." He turned away. "If I live I'll sell them." There was bitterness in his voice.

Chapter Twenty

DAVE FRANKLIN nursed his drink in Midway Store. In the passing weeks his face had thinned, and his large hands were even more calloused. Bad times had come to the Bend—as if things weren't bad enough before.

"It started the day we aimed to put the tar and feathers on Chase Iverton an' his wife," Franklin told Hugo Ortlander. "Things went bad from then on. Findin' some of my boys dead at the roundup camp. Findin' Ed and some of his cowhands shot. Things ain't no better since Dublin come back."

"I wasn't in favor of tar and featherin' a woman that day," Ortlander said grimly. "If you boys get the idea now I'll help you."

"I wouldn't dare even look sideways at her. Dublin's tough enough, but there's that runt Elmo Task. On top of that there's Luke Benreed."

"She's got Cross Hammer sure enough now."

"You mean Dublin's got it. They stood up before a travelin' preacher over at San Carlos the other day. She's Mrs. Paul Dublin now."

"I used to make a lot of excuses for Marie. But now I don't know."

Dave Franklin paid for his drink and pocketed the change. Since the death of Ed Bates he and his wife had taken in Mrs. Bates and the unmarried kids still at home. As if there weren't enough mouths to feed already. It was enough to turn a man's hair.

"My wife says it's high time they got married," Franklin said. "She says Marie's three months gone anyhow. I ain't seen her lately so I wouldn't know."

"You boys figure to trail a herd north?"

"We done wasted too much time waitin' for the colonel to come back. We never did know where he'd gone after Chase and that Mex took him outa roundup camp that night. Benreed said the colonel fell off a cliff somewheres in Mexico. And Chase got killed in a gunfight."

"You boys'll have to find another turncoat for your hot tar and feathers," Ortlander observed.

"I'd take Chase Iverton for a neighbor any day in place of Dublin and his crowd."

Ortlander poured a drink for Franklin. "On the house, Dave. I never figured I'd live long enough to hear you say anything good about Chase."

There was the sound of wagon wheels and a pounding of hoofs in the road. Both men turned and saw through the open door a spring wagon surrounded by half a dozen riders. Marie Iverton was in the wagon. It was driven by a plump Mexican woman.

"Speakin' of the devil," Ortlander said under his breath, as Dublin and Marie climbed the porch steps.

Paul Dublin swaggered in, a tight grin on his handsome face. "Break out a bottle, Hugo. That Pinchot's Reserve the colonel used to drink. Me an' Marie got hitched."

"So I heard," Ortlander said. He put the bottle on the bar.

Dublin and his men leaned their elbows on the bar. With him were Elmo Task and Benreed and three others who had been hired on recently. Dublin was already half-drunk. His boyish face was not quite so young as it had been before the trek into Mexico. But his smile was just as quick.

"I'm pushin' a herd north in three weeks," Dublin told Dave Franklin. "You pool boys want to go?"

"It's too late in the year," Franklin said. "You know that. You'll never beat the snow."

"Want to bet?" Dublin laughed. "My luck's on the upswing. Everything I do is right."

Franklin did not look at him. "Thanks for the drink, Hugo. See you next month."

He shuffled toward the door and Dublin, his face flaming, said, "Hold on there, Dave. I don't like a man's turnin' his back on me."

Franklin faced around. His large hands were clenched. The tip of a holster showed below his dirty threadbare canvas jacket. "I don't aim to trail a herd with you. This year or next."

There was a sudden quiet in the store. Marie looked up from a bolt of cloth she had been examining. Elmo Task stepped away from the bar. Dublin put a hand on his arm.

"Dave, you talk like a man who's got a hate on. You riled at me for some reason?" Dublin drawled.

Franklin stared across the dozen yards that separated them. A loose spring whirred in Ortlander's old brass wall clock. "I ain't forgot what we found at the Spur and Sixty-Six camp the mornin' after Chase Iverton made his break. We found a passel of dead men. Ed Bates shot in the gut—"

"Everybody knows it was a bunch of spics from across the line," Dublin said easily.

"Maybe." Again Franklin started for the door.

Dublin removed his hand from the arm of Elmo Task. "Shoot off his bootheels, Elmo. He walks too tall to suit me."

Task reached for his gun and at that moment Marie, carrying a bolt of cloth, stepped between the men at the bar and Franklin. She showed the cloth to her husband. "I think this would make a nice dress, Paul. What do you think?"

Dublin's eyes were bright. "I think next time you stay home. I don't like a woman buttin' in."

Task holstered the gun he had half drawn. Franklin was gone. There was the sound of a horse moving rapidly away from Midway Store. Hugo Ortlander's pale face was slick with sweat.

Marie carried the bolt of cloth back to the table.

After a moment of glaring at her slender back the tension went out of Dublin's shoulders. "Maybe it's a good thing she stepped in at that, Hugo. Be a shame to mess up your floor."

"Dave's a good man—"

"I always figured you was neutral, Hugo. You changin' your stripes?"

Ortlander said nothing for a moment while the Cross Hammer men watched him. Then he said, "You can't blame Dave for feelin' like he does. He lost a good friend in Bates that night. He lost some of his riders. He lost a lot of beef."

Dublin narrowed his gaze. He was drinking out of the bottle. Some of the whisky spilled down the front of his shirt. "Who do *you* think done the killin' and the thievin', Hugo?"

Ortlander spread his hands. He did not avert his gaze from the hard young face. "Like you said, I'm neutral."

Marie came over to the bar. "Hugo, we're spending the night. Do you have a room for us?"

"Sure, Marie." Ortlander's voice was tight with strain.

"You coming up soon, Paul?" she said.

"Sure." Dublin gave her his boyish smile. "You go along."

The men drank steadily. A few customers drifted in. By ten o'clock Dublin's eyes were bloodshot. Bloodshot and mean.

Ortlander sat on a stool behind his bar, looking nervous. Dublin never took his eyes off him even when he drank.

Dublin said, "You ain't neutral no more, Hugo."

"Yes, I am," the little man said quickly. "I told you I am."

"No more. You're Cross Hammer. You don't let none of them pool scum in the door. You hear?"

"They're my friends."

Dublin shifted his gaze to Benreed down the bar. "Luke, you ever pitch horseshoes?"

"When I was a kid."

"Pitch Hugo a little," Dublin said, grinning. "I want to hear him come up shoutin' Viva Cross Hammer."

Flexing his thick arms Benreed went behind the bar. Ortlander, a frightened squeak breaking from his lips, tried to reach a gun. Benreed took it away from him. He picked Ortlander up in his two hands and held him over his head.

"Don't—don't—don't—" Ortlander was waving his hands wildly.

"Like this?" Benreed said, grinning at Dublin.

He pitched Ortlander against the wall. The little man fell loosely. His head was twisted at an odd angle.

"Get up, Hugo," Dublin said thickly. "Get up."

He walked over. Benreed was staring down at Ortlander. There was a break in the skin just below the right ear. It was bleeding.

Dublin touched the skull with his boot and rolled it back and forth. He looked at Benreed accusingly. "You throwed him too hard. His neck is busted."

Benreed rubbed a hand over his jaw. "You said pitch him an' I did."

"There oughta be a shovel in the barn," Dublin said. "You boys fix him a hole in the ground. I got to go upstairs. You know how it is when a man's got a bride a waitin' for him."

Laughing he swayed across the room on his built-up heels and drunkenly climbed the stairs.

When he was in bed Marie said, "What was that noise downstairs a few minutes ago?"

"Hugo knocked over a flour barrel." He turned to her. "I'm movin' down to Flatiron tomorrow for a couple of weeks. Want to come?"

"No. What are you going to do there?"

"Makin' a quick gather. You're Chase's widow. You own his cows. I aim to push 'em to Kansas with the Cross Hammer herd."

"All right, Paul."

He chuckled. "I ain't mad at you, honey. I'm glad you stopped Elmo from makin' that fool play with Franklin."

"Paul, sometimes you frighten me."

"Oh, hell, we was just goin' to have a little fun."

"Paul, our lives are different now. We'll have a child to raise."

"Let the Mex woman raise him. Soon's we sell that herd you an' me are goin' to Frisco an'—"

"This child is yours, Paul. If it's a boy won't you have any pride in him at all?"

Dublin was snoring.

She lay in the dark for a long time, thinking of the night she and Chase had occupied this room for the last time. Remembering how her father had smashed in the door. And now her father lay dead in some canyon in Mexico. And Chase was dead. And— She felt the tears. She felt older than anyone else on earth.

Old and alone.

But in the months to come she would never be alone again. Never in her life. She could close her eyes against this man she had married and pretend the things he did were of no consequence. They could not touch her again.

Nothing could touch her. Or her child.

She would have her child and nothing else mattered.

Chapter Twenty-one

CHASE DROVE each day with Red to Jessie's cottage. There they would take their meals and he would sit in the sun and talk. One day in the hotel room Red said, "Maybe you figured I had no business buttin' in with you an' Jessie—"

"You're Jessie's friend. It's good enough reason for me."

"I knowed Jessie most since she was born. I knowed her pa and all the boys. I was there the day her crazy brother Mike got his leg shot off fightin' over a woman that had alley cat blood in her veins. I— Well, you see I feel that I got to sorta look out after her. Now if you two was fixin' to marry I'd soon quit fussin'—"

"Red, I'm already married."

"I figured somethin' like that. Does Jessie know?"

"Yes."

"I knowed a fella once that got a dee-vorce."

"I'm going to find my wife and the man she ran off with. I'm going to kill him. Maybe I'll have to kill others. Probably." He sighed. "Jessie's had enough killing in her life. I'm not going to ask her to wait for me. Because my hands will be bloodied to the elbows if I come back at all. Either way I'd bring her more grieving."

Red cleared his throat. "Reckon I'll go up to the mine. We'll have first snow one of these days. I'll close her down for the winter and come back."

"I probably won't be here."

"Good luck, Iverton. Good luck in your killing."

Chase stared out the window thinking, I started my search for Marie in the spring. And now it is almost winter. He crossed the room and stared at his reflection in the looking glass nailed to the wall. Jessie's cooking had filled out his face. But there was something in his eyes that had not been there before he started the search for the woman he married.

Chase walked out into the darkness. Overhead the stars were sharp as points of steel against the sky. He smelled the dampness of the river and heard its whispers. Windows were filled with lamplight and somewhere a girl laughed softly. He looked in the direction of Jessie's house but the distance was too great and he was glad. He owed it to her to leave. To get out of her life.

They'd had much together. They'd nearly died together.

But he already had a wife. And he had a debt to settle.

That afternoon he had talked with a teamster stopping over in Rivertown. Now he hunted up this man. In the first light he was riding with the freight outfit. He had no money and his stomach cried out at its emptiness.

In Paso Del Norte he listened to the excited talk. The war in Mexico was about over. Maximilian was on the run. He wondered what had happened to Captain Morellos. When he thought of this man and the burned-out village by the river he turned cold.

He moved on shaky legs along the crowded street until he came to a sign: J. MYERS. LAND. CATTLE.

In a second floor office he shook the hand of a small, bald man wearing a faded green vest. "You knew my father," Chase said. "Before the war. My name is Iverton."

"Your father? I remember him well."

"Mr. Myers, I own Flatiron Ranch free and clear. I don't have papers with me, but I need a loan. I want a crew. They won't work for nothing. A thousand dollars would get me back in the cattle business."

"Chase, your father was a dreamer. So are you." The little man fussed with some papers on his dust-covered desk. "I wouldn't loan a thousand dollars on the state of Texas."

"I'll have over a thousand head of beef."

"Not even a dollar a head would I loan. In the first place I don't have that much cash. We've had a war, boy. And things are black and looking no better."

"But there's a beef market in Kansas."

"Ah. There you have a different story." Myers leaned

forward. "Beef in Kansas means hard Yankee money. Beef in Texas means not one damn thing."

"I'll take a herd north in the spring."

"Come to think of it didn't I hear that you married Herrick's daughter?"

Chase looked out a fly-specked window into the street below where a freighter, water barrels lashed to its sideboards, headed toward Mexico. "Yes, I married her."

Myers studied the face that had regained some of its color in the sun at Rivertown. "Chase, you look like a man who's had a long illness."

"Illness? Yes, you might call it that."

Myers regarded him shrewdly. "An illness induced by a bullet wound, maybe."

Chase shrugged.

"You want money and men to go after whoever it was that shot you."

"You could get rich telling fortunes."

"Chase, I'll loan you two hundred dollars. You don't have to sign a damn thing. Shake my hand. It's good enough for me."

With money in his pocket Chase paused at the door. "What news do you hear from the Bend?"

"News from there is always five years late. That's the loneliest spot in the world. Don't you remember?"

"Thanks, Myers, for the loan."

That evening he rode east and south, mounted on a good horse he'd picked up at an auction. He had a new outfit; hat, shirt, pants, boots. In his saddle scabbard was a rifle. At his belt he carried a revolver.

For the first time in months he felt whole again.

Finally he came to Midway Store. First he made sure there were no saddlers at the rail before he entered. The familiar room with its disorder. The short bar. The stairway leading to the upstairs rooms.

He felt a warmth. A man he did not know came out of a back room. A tall man with a fringe of black hair. He wore a dirty apron.

"Howdy, stranger," the man said.

"Where's Hugo?"

"He ain't here. My wife an' I was lookin' for a place to put a little money an' we bought this. Nice peaceful place. We used to run the *tienda* in San Carlos. Bought it in April an' sold it last month. Made a profit, too."

"It doesn't seem right that Hugo would sell this place. Where'd he go?"

"Mexico. He's got a sister livin' down there."

"Hugo's got no kin. No kin in the world."

The man's jaw dropped. "All I know is what the fella said that sold me this place. Hugo owed him some money an' he took it over."

"What fella?"

"Paul Dublin—"

Chase turned on his heel and walked to the door. He looked back. "We'll talk some more about this, mister."

As soon as he had gone a woman came from the back room. She was pale as death. She was in her forties, a widow. Last spring she had married Reese Bishop, who now owned Midway Store.

Now Bishop turned and said to his wife, "That fella sure acted funny. Claimed Ortlander never had no kin—"

"Mother of God," the woman breathed. "That was Chase Iverton."

"Who's he— Oh, you mean the one that got killed in Mexico?" His eyes opened wider. "That means Marie Dublin ain't Marie Dublin at all. She's Marie Iverton—"

"Listen, Reese. I've lived around here all my life. We've got every dime of our savings in this store. We'll lose everything—"

"Wait a minute, Martha. You don't make sense."

"I learned years ago if you live in the Bend you play with the big ones. Or you don't live. And there's nothing bigger than Cross Hammer. Reese, you take off that apron and ride to Cross Hammer. You tell 'em that Chase Iverton was here today at Midway Store."

"From what I hear the name Iverton is a lot more respected around here in spite of him bein' a turncoat, than is the name Dublin—"

"You listen to me, Reese!" The woman was screaming. "I know what I'm talking about. You play Cross Hammer's game, you understand?"

"I'm my own man. I paid Dublin for this store an' I got me a bill-of-sale—"

"Do you want them to maybe burn this place down on our heads?"

"They wouldn't dare. The law—"

"You tell me about the law, Reese," she said, her voice shaking. "I ain't never heard of law around here since before the war. So you tell me."

"I dunno, Martha. I don't like to mix in nothin' that ain't my business."

The woman clutched her husband's arm and looked fearfully around the big empty store as if hunting for possible eavesdroppers. "I was pokin' around behind the barn yesterday. In some soft dirt. I got curious. I done some diggin'. There's a man buried there."

Her husband's eyes widened in disbelief. "What man?"

"I dunno. I was scared to look. But after what Iverton said, an' thinkin' it over—Reese, Ortlander never had a sister in Mexico. I should've known better."

Reese Bishop went white. "You mean—"

"I'll bet my last gold hairpin the man out there is Ortlander."

Bishop slowly untied his apron. He looked ill. "I don't cotton to that bunch of hellions at Cross Hammer. But maybe you're right. I guess we got to protect ourselves."

"Somebody might have seen Iverton in here. Or seen him on the road here and they'll know darn well he'd come in and say howdy to his old friend Ortlander. And Dublin might ask us why we didn't spread the word. I don't want anything to happen to you, Reese. I don't want you layin' out behind somebody's barn."

"How far is it to Cross Hammer, you reckon?"

"About fifteen miles. You better hurry."

Chapter Twenty-two

CHASE TOOK his time. He kept off the road. Once he saw riders in the distance but they passed without observing him. The day was young. He thought of the times he and Marie had come along the road he now paralleled. Who was Marie? he asked himself. How did her mouth feel? Was her hair soft to the touch like Jessie's? It was such a distant thing in his mind that it was lost.

At last he looked down upon the mud-walled buildings of Flatiron. There were a half dozen horses in one of his corrals. The other holding corral was empty. The gate was missing from the stone breaking corral. He thought of his dreams of selling horses to Fort Ellenden. Dreams as dead now as the dust under his boots.

A column of smoke drifted lazily from the rock chimney of the house. A man left his home for a spell, he thought, and somebody moved in. That was the way it seemed to be in Texas these days.

For two hours he sat in the shade of a rock outcropping and watched the buildings below. Once a fat man came to the door and emptied a pan of water into the yard.

If there was anyone else around they kept out of sight. Even though the distance was great Chase had the feeling there was something familiar about the fat man. Fat Enfield was one of the old hands at Cross Hammer, who stayed on through the war.

What was one of the Cross Hammer crew doing here? If it really was Enfield, that is.

Gauging the wind, he moved toward the east where he could come down from the heights and keep the barn between himself and the house. It was also downwind from the horses in the corral.

Some fifty yards from the barn he left his horse where mesquites grew high. He crept forward on foot, rifle hammer under his thumb. At a corner of the barn he halted and peered at the house. Still nothing moved. He picked up a stone and threw it against the front door.

Instantly the door jerked open. The fat man came running out. He held a rifle and looked wildly around. It was Fat Enfield all right. He wore a dirty hat and apron. His belly was big as a sack of river sand.

After a moment of peering suspiciously around the yard Enfield started back into the house.

"Hold it, Enfield," Chase said loudly.

For a moment the man stood rigid. Chase was ready to cut his fat legs from under him if the man tried to bolt for the house.

"This is Chase Iverton! Drop that rifle and turn around!"

Enfield shuddered as if hit in the back with a club.

He let the rifle fall. He faced around, his face going white. "My gawd," he said in a shocked voice when he saw the man by the barn. "They claimed you was dead."

"Not very dead." Chase came up slowly, rifle centered on the fat belly. "You alone?"

"Yeah—yeah, I'm alone." Enfield's voice shook.

Prodding the fat man in front of him Chase searched the barn, the shed. And finally the house. Nothing had changed, save that it was dirtier. The pan was filled with unwashed dishes and the floor hadn't been swept. It was as if Marie still lived here. Along one wall was riding gear, saddles, boots, bridles. Two big pots were steaming on the stove. The small stove where Marie had shown so little talent.

Enfield was sweating. "Nobody ever figured to see you again, Iverton."

"I shouldn't wonder. You're trespassing. This is my ranch!"

"Paul said—" Enfield's Adam's apple made a surprising sweep up his fat neck then swiftly descended. There was something in Chase Iverton's gaze that turned a man to ice. "Don't look at me like that! I only work for Dublin. I got nothin' to say about what goes on."

Chase questioned the quavering fat man. Flatiron was being used as a line camp. Paul Dublin, Benreed and Elmo Task were with some of the Cross Hammer crew a few miles south. They were rounding up Flatiron cows, intending to push them north to Cross Hammer.

"Paul will be back here tonight?" Chase said.

"Yeah." Enfield licked his fat lips. "You better light out while you got the chance, Iverton. They're too many for you."

"Where is my wife?"

"Mrs. Dublin—I mean Mrs. Iverton, I mean— Oh, hell, she's livin' at Cross Hammer."

"I wish she could witness me killing Paul," Chase said to himself more than to Enfield.

"So you kill Paul," Enfield said. "The rest of 'em will tear you to pieces."

"I'm praying Paul will ride here alone. Or that I can find him somewhere alone."

"You're loco, Iverton. You got no chance at all. Even if

you get Paul and Luke Benreed, maybe. There's still Elmo Task. That runt is hell's wheels with a gun."

"Last time I was here there was a dead man in the yard," Chase said grimly. "Did you see anything of a body when you came here?"

There had been a skeleton by the barn, Enfield admitted. Paul Dublin ordered it thrown in the weeds.

"You're going to spend the next hour digging a grave," Chase said.

Despite the fat man's protests Chase made him get a blanket from the house and wrap the remains of Miguel Arguello in it. The fat man sweated and cursed as he shoveled the hard Texas soil.

Standing by the open grave Chase tried to remember a prayer. But his mind seemed empty. "This man saved my life," he said. "Dear Lord, please treat him kindly."

After the digging of the grave Enfield huddled on the ground, utterly spent. Chase started to haul him to his feet but at that moment he caught sight of a plume of dust moving toward them from the north. Enfield had said Dublin and the rest were working south of Flatiron headquarters.

Enfield had also seen the dust. "Maybe it's some of the boys down from Cross Hammer," he said hopefully.

Chase thought of the horse that he had left some fifty yards behind the barn. The wise thing to do was run for it. But he was past running. Besides, now at second glance, he saw the dust cloud was small. Two riders, maybe. Then as he watched the road he saw that the dust had been raised by a buckboard and team. The driver was a woman. As the rig neared he could see pale hair. Marie. She was alone.

Seizing Enfield by an arm Chase hustled him into the barn. Hastily he cut up an old saddle rope and used the short ends to tie the fat man. He shoved him in a corner. Just as he stepped outside Marie pulled the buckboard into the yard.

When she saw Chase she sat rigidly a moment. Then in sudden desperation she tried to whip up the team. But he had been running and now he jerked the lines from her hands. Hauling back he brought the team to a halt and tied it. There was a carbine on the floorboards but she made no attempt to reach it.

"You don't seem surprised to see me," he said.

"Reese Bishop rode over from Midway Store. He said you had been there. I came down to warn Paul."

"Why didn't you bring the whole crew?"

She said nothing to this. He caught her by a wrist and forced her to step down from the buckboard. She wore a buttoned, loose-fitting blue coat.

"So you call yourself Mrs. Dublin," he said.

"Paul and I were married."

He gave her a hard smile. "How was it with you and Paul in Mexico?"

"I was lonely and frightened."

"Funny, but that's the way you put it the first time we saw each other after the war. And I took pity on you. I married you."

"You said you loved me."

"Pity is sometimes a watered-down version of love." He marched her into the house they had shared together. The iron lids on the pots began to rattle as steam made its escape.

He looked at her closely. Around her eyes and nostrils were incipient lines. She looked older, harder at the mouth.

"Why?" Chase said. "Tell me one good reason why you went with him."

"Paul didn't treat me gentle. I guess a firm hand is what I needed."

"It doesn't make me look like much of a man."

"You're a gentleman. Paul isn't."

"Not now am I a gentleman. All that ended the night I came home and found you gone."

"Can't you understand?" She was clenching, unclenching her pale hands. "I thought you were dead."

Chase bared his teeth. "I guess all along I knew what Paul was. Even when we were boys. But when you're raised with a man you make allowances. He's done well by me. He not only stole my horses and my wife. Now I understand he intends to steal my cows."

"We thought you were dead. I'll see that every cow is returned to you."

"So considerate of you, Mrs. Dublin."

She sank into a chair and put a hand across her eyes. "You're going after Paul." It was a statement, not a question.

"He's lived too long."

She tried suddenly to grasp his hands, but he withdrew them. "Chase, listen to me. Killing Paul won't solve anything. He's the only thing I ever had in my whole life. I loved him first, Chase. Long before you."

"I was a fool bridegroom. But not so big a fool that I didn't know. So it was Paul."

"Even if you managed to kill him, you'd never live."

"My pleasure in his dying outweighs the risks."

For a moment she said nothing. Then she unbuttoned the coat and pulled it away from her lap. He saw the swelling there. His mouth was ugly.

"You wasted no time," he said thinly, and wanted to hit her in the face.

"Chase, I was never right for you. It—" She closed her eyes. "If my baby is a girl I hope she'll be a better woman than her mother. If it's a boy I hope he'll hurt fewer people than my father did. Or Paul did."

"Your father died searching for you. I nearly died. Aren't you a little late with this sort of talk?"

"Poppa ruined his life with hatred. Don't ruin yours."

"And I'm supposed to forget my own hurt. Just so long as I don't hurt you. Or hurt Paul."

"What will it gain to kill him?"

"Satisfaction." ·

"At what a price. The price of your own life."

"This child you're going to bear is supposed to soften me, is that it? I'm supposed to forget what you and Paul have done."

"Let me tell you something. People around here think more of you than they do of Paul and me. They despise us. I know. You can tell the way people look at you." She looked at him for a long moment. One of the kettles boiled over but they paid no attention. "Paul will do whatever I ask him to."

"That I doubt."

"In this one thing he will. We'll sell Cross Hammer. We'll go away and you'll never hear of us again. You can divorce me. Then Paul and I will be married." Her chin trembled. "Do this one thing for me."

He crossed the room and stood looking at the distant hills. He thought of Jessie waiting for him. He turned and looked around at the woman hunched in a chair. She was a stranger. She was someone he had never seen before. A faint hope began to climb in him.

He didn't want to die. He wanted to live—for Jessie. How quickly the tension seemed to drain out of him. Should he ride away from the killings and go back to Jessie? Say that because of knowing her he could not bring himself to kill this man who had wronged him.

That might bring him Jessie. But would he ever again find peace within himself?

And with the draining away of tension he felt a weakness in his legs. He knew that despite his boast to Fat Enfield he was in no condition to face Paul and Paul's men. He might kill Paul. He might be lucky enough to down Luke Benreed. But the rest of them would shoot him to pieces. He would have his revenge and Jessie would have her memory of a brief but tragic courtship.

He suddenly made up his mind. "You talk to Paul. I don't think he'll calmly sell Cross Hammer and go away, but—"

"Chase, you'll see." Her face was bright and she hurried across the room and touched his arm. "You're a good man. You were always much too good for me."

"I'll pull out of here for a week. Put Cross Hammer up for sale. You and Paul go away. If he doesn't agree to this I'll get men somewhere. I'll come back and wipe Cross Hammer off the map of Texas."

"You'll never regret giving me this chance." She followed him to the door. "I could have brought the crew from Cross Hammer, or sent them when I heard you were back in the Bend. But I didn't. I came to talk to Paul. To get him to agree that fighting you was useless. So you see even before you came I wanted peace between you and Paul."

"All right. Like I said, you try and talk to him."

"I'll wait here for Paul. We'll have our talk tonight and be gone in the morning."

He turned out of the house, wondering if he was right. Or was he showing weakness. But what else to do? You don't kill the woman who has double-crossed you. You

can't horsewhip her even if the urge is strong in you.
Especially not when she's carrying a child.

Paul's child!

For a moment the old rage surged through him
again. But Jessie's image was also in his consciousness.
And this outweighed his hatred.

When he got to the barn he found that Enfield had
managed to saw through his bonds by rubbing them over
a rusty nail projecting from the wall.

Chapter Twenty-three

THERE WAS A faint dull throbbing at his temples as he
stared down at the rope ends that lay on the floor of the
barn. Numbly he walked to the rear door and peered
toward the mesquites where he had left his horse. The
horse was gone.

Rifle under his arm he followed Enfield's running foot-
prints to the mesquites. He saw where Enfield had
walked the horse for some distance then set it to a gal-
lop.

A half hour ago he would have welcomed the sight
of Paul riding in. Never mind that Paul had ten men
with him or twenty. But now the urge to live was strong
in him again. All because of Jessie.

He turned back into the mesquites intending to rope
a horse from the corral. He'd get one of the saddles out
of the house. In ten minutes he'd be gone.

But he had taken no more than half a dozen steps
when he heard the far off pound of hoofbeats. They were
coming from the south where Enfield said Paul had gone
this day with his men.

Chase glanced toward the house, seeing through the
fringe of mesquites that Marie had also heard the approach of riders. She was in the yard, looking south,
shielding her eyes against the afternoon glare.

No time to get a horse now. He felt his mouth jerk.
This was it. The test for Marie. If she held as much in-

fluence over Paul as she thought, then the thing would end peacefully, with them riding off. If she double-crossed him again, or if she did not have that influence, then there would be dead men in the yard.

And a dead man here in the mesquites, he thought with a hollow sinking sensation in his stomach.

In a moment he knew from the sound of the hard-ridden horses that there were only a few riders approaching. Not the whole crew. Be thankful for small favors, he told himself. It might not even be Paul, but some of the men working nearby that Enfield had encountered first.

Now he could see three riders coming across the flats at a dead run. Even at this distance he recognized Paul Dublin's slender figure in the lead, the wind pushing up the brim of his hat. Flanking him and a little behind were the diminutive, lethal Elmo Task and Luke Benreed. Benreed rode with rifle in hand, a big tough-looking man. As they swept by the mesquites Chase thought of all Dublin had done. Remembered how Benreed had shot Miguel Arguello in the back.

His hands were slick on the rifle. How simple to settle this score with three rifle bullets. Knock the trio kicking from their horses. Killing Paul and Benreed would give him satisfaction. Killing Elmo Task would mean nothing, save that a threat to his life would be removed.

Three of them against one. Unless Marie kept her word. And if she kept her word would Paul listen. If anything at all would change Paul perhaps it was the fact that he was soon to be a father.

The three men reined in sharply before the house and Dublin's voice came clearly from the yard: "We was on our way in. Enfield caught us. Where's Chase?"

Marie shouted, "Listen to me, Paul!"

They were dismounting. Benreed and Task stood apart from Marie and Paul Dublin. Both men held rifles and were looking toward the barn and the shed.

Marie was talking earnestly to Dublin. He wore a bulky sheepskin jacket. Because of the distance Chase could not hear their animated conversation. He saw Dublin give an emphatic shake of his head and start away from Marie. She ran to catch him and the unbuttoned coat ballooned away from her swollen body.

She was weeping. "Paul! Paul, listen to me—"

But when she caught him by the arm with both hands he gave her a shove. But still she clung to his arm. A taut angry look crossed his face and he cursed wildly. He shifted his rifle to his left hand. Deliberately he lifted his right hand then sent it crashing against her face. The force of the blow knocked Marie to her knees. While the three men watched her with varying emotions on their faces, Paul started to walk away from the woman. She fell forward, caught him by a leg. In order to retain his balance he was forced to make several hopping steps.

With his free leg he kicked back viciously. A low cry of pain came from Marie as the heel of his boot caught her. She crumpled up on the hard Texas ground. She did not move.

In that moment Chase thought, Run with the wolves, and one day you'll feel their fangs.

Ignoring the woman on the ground Paul walked over to where Benreed and Task were standing.

Dublin said sharply, "Chase is around here somewheres. Enfield's got his horse. And there's the same bunch in the corral there was when we left this mornin'. So that means he didn't take one of those. He's afoot. Likely holed up in the barn yonder."

Chase, moving quietly from the mesquites to the barn, heard Benreed say, "How many times you got to shoot Iverton to make him stay dead?"

"Shoot him in the legs," Dublin snarled. He was shrugging out of his heavy jacket. He put down his rifle and drew his revolver. "I want Marie to watch him hang."

Elmo Task had been staring at Dublin. And now Dublin said, "What the hell's chewin' on you, Elmo?"

"I seen lots of things. I never seen a man kick a woman before."

"I didn't hurt her none," Dublin said quickly. "I'll tend to her once we're shet of Chase."

Without a word Task picked up the jacket. Dublin had dropped. He carried it across the yard in his right hand, rifle in the other. When he came to where Marie lay so still upon the ground he started to cover her with the jacket.

Task shifted the rifle under his right arm. He stood

hunched over the woman on the ground for what seemed like an age.

Dublin looked around at him. "Tell her I didn't mean to kick her. I lost my head. Come on, let's get Chase." Dublin stiffened a little. "You with me, Elmo?"

Slowly Task straightened up. He dropped the jacket.

"You son of a bitch," Task said, and let the rifle fall by lifting his arm. In the same movement he tried to reach his belt gun. He got it out of its holster, but Dublin had only to drop the hammer of his revolver.

The solid crashing sound from the revolver. Elmo Task sagged. The second shot sent him reeling. He fell, rolled. Still retaining his grip on his revolver, Task tried to center it on his target. Dublin shot him again. This time when Task fell back all movement was gone from him.

"I never seen a snake so hard to kill," Dublin said, sweating. He swiftly reloaded his gun.

Benreed looked back at Task lying upon the ground. "He sure went loco all of a sudden."

"Yeah."

"You still want to shoot Iverton in the legs?"

"Hell no. Kill him!"

Under the cover of the firing Chase had sprinted the remaining distance to the corner of the barn. Now he began inching along the wall. Discarding his rifle he drew the belt gun. This was short gun work. He wanted to shoot Paul in the gut. He wanted him to take a long time in dying.

Paul Dublin was shouting, "Chase, come outa the barn. Or we'll burn it!"

Chase appeared suddenly around a corner of the barn. Dublin was moving toward the barn door. Benreed was beside him. It was Dublin who caught sight of Chase first. His shot was hurried and Chase dodged it.

Caught by surprise at Chase's sudden appearance, Benreed snapped off a shot. But Chase was falling to one side. He let the gun hammer slip out from under his thumb. The bullet struck Benreed in the neck. A muscle must have been severed for Benreed's head tilted queerly. He fell forward against the barn wall and seemed to break in two. His face scraped the rough planks all the way to the ground.

During this exchange Dublin had tried to reach the shelter of the barn. Wanting him alive, not dead, Chase tried to shoot him in the leg. Instead his bullet shattered Dublin's right ankle. Dublin fell, screaming.

As Chase started to run forward his left leg folded up. As he was falling he realized numbly that one of the bullets had struck him in the thigh. Dazedly he picked himself up, limped to where Dublin lay. Dublin lay with his legs drawn up. Dublin seemed gripped with shock. Three feet away his gun was gleaming in the dust. Chase kicked it out of reach. Dublin sat up, his face white. A hole in the right boot, cut by the heavy caliber slug, was leaking his blood.

Making sure Benreed was dead and Dublin unarmed, Chase staggered to where Elmo Task lay curled up on the ground. The little man did not move. The front of his shirt was darkly stained.

Fighting nausea because of the pain and shock Chase limped to Marie. One look was all he needed. He wanted to throw up.

He reeled to one of the three horses that stood, reins trailed, whites of the eyes showing. The scent of blood was strong to them and they moved nervously. It took two tries before Chase was able to get a saddle rope from the nearest horse.

Then he dragged himself back to where Dublin was hunched on the ground. Dublin seemed nearly out. Chase dropped a noose over Dublin's head and drew it tight.

The feel of the rope about his neck brought Dublin back from the edge of darkness. His hands shot to the rope and tried to loosen it. Chase drew it tighter.

"Get up and walk!" Chase cried.

"I can't—my ankle!"

"Walk! Goddam it, walk!"

With all his strength he pulled on the rope. He began to drag Dublin inch by inch across the yard.

At last he got him over to where Marie lay so quietly.

"Look at her!" Chase cried, and his voice was shaking.

"Jeezus," Dublin managed to mutter.

"I never meant to hurt Marie like that—"

"You never were any good, Paul! You're a murderer twice over. You killed her. You killed her child!"

He hauled Dublin to the barn, limping every step. He left a trail of his own blood on the ground. Desperately Dublin tried to fight him. Once he hit Dublin in the face. After that it was hauling a dead weight. But so great was his purpose that he managed this.

Inside the barn he threw the end of the rope over a low rafter. He hauled on it with all his weight. Dublin screamed. The pain of his ankle, the knifing of the rope at his throat had brought him around and he fought savagely with all this strenth. But Chase kept out of his way. Chase heaved hard on the rope and this brought Dublin up short.

Finally Chase was able to tie the rope end to the corner of a slatted feed bin. He paused then, drawing a shaky breath. There was the sound of a great roaring tide in his ears. He staggered to the spot where Fat Enfield had freed himself earlier. With two short lengths of rope in his hand Chase limped back to where Dublin stood under the barn rafter. Dublin was unable to move because of the tautness of the rope.

Quickly Chase fought one of Dublin's wrists to the belt and tied it. Then he tied the other.

Dublin glared at him. He stood on one foot, his wrists tied. He was sweating. Pain was mixed with hatred in his eyes.

Finally he said, "For God's sake, Chase. I never meant to kick her."

"She trusted you. She said she had influence over you."

It took all of his will power to drag up a large wooden box. As he came close Dublin tried to tear at his face with his teeth. Chase slapped him hard across the mouth. The force of the blow nearly cost Dublin his balance. A wild fear was bright in his eyes as he sagged against the rope. But by hopping on one foot he regained his balance. Chase got behind him and lifted him by the knees. He managed to boost Dublin onto the box. And at the same moment with his left hand, he took up the slack in the rope slung over the rafter. Keeping the tension on the rope he limped over to the feed bin and tightened it.

When this was done Chase sagged against the wall. He looked at Dublin who stood on the box, rope tight at his throat. No slack in the rope at all. Dublin, balancing himself on his good foot. His face was gray. Blood from the twisted ankle dripped down onto straw, making bright stars of color on faded yellow.

"One question," Chase gasped. "Hugo Ortlander. What happened to him?"

"Cut me loose and I'll tell you!"

"You killed him."

"No. Benreed—"

"When I kick that box óut from under you," Chase panted, "I want you to think of every damn dirty thing you ever did."

Tears ran down Paul Dublin's face. His hat was gone. His curly hair, damp with sweat, was matted against his skull. His clothing was torn, dusty from his being dragged across the yard.

"I never meant to hurt Marie!" Dublin cried.

"Paul, I wish to God I could hang you twice."

Dublin's mouth sagged. "Chase, hear me out. Cut me down. Give me a gun with one bullet in it. I'll blow out my brains."

"Or blow out mine if I was fool enough to turn my back."

"It was love with me an' Marie. She loved me all the time, Chase. I—"

Chase suddenly felt old and tired and sickened. He limped to the barn door. As if sensing a weakness in Chase, Dublin cried, "You ain't got the guts to kick this box out from under me!"

Chase looked back at this man he had known for so many years. "How long do you think you can stand on one leg?"

He went out into the yard. Instantly he was caught up short. There was something wrong. He shook his head violently from side to side. Had his wound brought about a weakness in vision? He looked again.

Elmo Task was gone.

"Behind you, Iverton."

Chase reached for his gun. His hand was so ungodly slow it was pitiful. He turned and there sat Elmo Task. The little man had dragged himself to the barn. He sat on the ground, his back to the wall.

Task held a gun, cocked. Held it in his left hand. His

right arm was bleeding badly. There was a hole in the front of his shirt near the collarbone. Another hole was lower down.

"I got nothin' against you, Iverton," Task said in a voice tight from pain and weakness. "I worked for Dublin. I got no boss now."

"Dublin isn't dead. Not yet."

A smile flickered across the little man's lips. "Like you already told him. A man can't stand on one foot forever."

Chase stood with hands spread wide from his body. A numbness enveloped his whole body. "What now?" he managed to gasp.

"We're both shot up. I've sat my last saddle. You better set an' rest yourself. You know how to pray, Iverton?"

"I learned how after I was shot in Mexico."

"Pray that I live till the boys get here. I'll tell 'em about Paul. And what he done to his wife."

There was a thud from inside the barn. A man's scream was cut brutally short.

The men from Cross Hammer rode in a quarter of an hour later. There were fifteen of them including Fat Enfield. They listened to the telling of the brutal thing Paul Dublin had done.

The men were hard of eye, unsentimental usually. But when Task finished the telling there was sadness on some of the faces.

"Killin' a woman an' her unborn kid," Fat Enfield breathed. "I never heard tell of nothin' like that."

A few of them went into the barn and looked at Paul Dublin hanging by his neck. And one of them spit in his dead face.

They had no jobs now, no one to pay their salaries. And there was no loyalty to Cross Hammer.

They took time to dig one large grave behind the barn. The other grave was smaller and on a knoll near the house.

Into the large grave they put Benreed, Elmo Task and Paul Dublin. The other grave was for Marie.

A couple of the Cross Hammer men nodded at Chase and wished him luck. Then they all rode out.

Chase could hobble about the yard on his stiffened

leg. He had one lucky break. The bullet had gone clear through without hitting bone.

After the men had gone he knocked loose one of the planks from the barn wall. He cut into the seasoned wood with the point of a knife. He carved a name—Marie. For a long time he debated what other name to put after it, whether Dublin or Iverton. But Paul Dublin did not deserve to have his name perpetuated in any form.

And did she ever really belong to me? Chase thought.

He finished the carving and set the plank on the knoll near the house. It said:

MARIE HERRICK
1845 — 1866

He wanted to wait a few days before sitting a saddle, so he loafed around, cleaning up the house, putting things away.

At the end of the week four riders appeared. Chase, rifle hammer under his thumb, stepped to the yard. It was Dave Franklin and three of his men.

"Figure to paint 'turncoat' on my barn again?" Chase said thinly.

"We heard what happened," Franklin said. He cleared his throat awkwardly. "Pretty late in the year to trail a herd to Kansas. But I'm goin' in the spring. Wondered if you wanted to go with us. Me an' my neighbors—your neighbors—would admire to have you."

"We'll talk about it, Dave. But first I've got a long ride ahead of me."

"Ride? To where?"

"Rivertown."

He arrived there the following week. He dismounted in front of Jessie's house, the place where he had fought his way back to life.

The door opened and Jessie stood there. "I knew you'd come."

"You hate violence, Jessie. I had some killing to do."

"I still hate violence. But my love for you is stronger than any other feeling." She came quickly down the porch steps. Her eyes were shining.

"Things might've worked out peacefully, but—"

"You don't have to tell me. Some of the Cross Hammer riders were through here on their way to New Mexico. The story is all over town. I'm sorry about your wife."

They walked arm in arm into the house.

"Flatiron isn't much, Jessie. It has a dirt floor and the stove is propped up on 'dobe bricks. There's only one room. But I can add on."

"What difference does it make? One room or ten. If people who care about each other are together that's all that counts."

"Jessie, I never started to live until I met you."

"Let's go find Red and tell him."

"First I've got things to tell you," and smiling, he kicked the door shut behind him.